A MURDER FOR
HER MAJESTY

A MURDER FOR HER MAJESTY

Beth Hilgartner

Houghton Mifflin Company
Boston

Library of Congress Cataloging-in-Publication Data

Hilgartner, Beth.
   A murder for Her Majesty.

   Summary: Horrified at having witnessed her father's
murder and fearing that the killers are agents of
Queen Elizabeth I, eleven-year-old Alice Tuckfield
hides in the Yorkshire cathedral by disguising herself
as one of the choirboys.
   [1. Cathedrals—Fiction. 2. Choirboy training—
Fiction. 3.Yorkshire—Fiction. 4. England—Social
life and customs—16th century—Fiction] I. Title.
PZ7.H5474Mu 1986   [Fic]   86-10316
ISBN 0-395-41451-2
PA ISBN 0-395-61619-0

Printed in the United States of America

QUM 20 19 18 17 16 15

For John,
who gave me Byrd

Acknowledgments

I would like to thank all the people at the Granite Bank, especially Jamie and Sue, for their understanding, support, and the use of the computer.

A MURDER FOR
HER MAJESTY

CHAPTER ONE

Alice was cold. Though the rain had stopped, her wet cloak was little shield against the bitter November wind. She was also tired and very, very hungry. Bewildered by the narrow streets of the Shambles, she wandered aimlessly. She had hoped to find the cathedral where the kind old woman with the dried flowers had told her she might find food and shelter. The directions had been complicated and she hadn't paid too much attention, for she thought it would be a simple matter to find the cathedral — just follow the tower — but she had reckoned without the tall houses that leaned out over the narrow streets and obscured her view. She had tried several times to ask directions, but she could get none of the hurrying people to take any notice of her.

She bit her lip and fought back tears. Crying would do no good. Her destination, Chellisford Hall, was nearly eight miles outside York; it might as well be in London, she thought, for all the chance she had of reaching it tonight. Soon it would be dark. If she couldn't find the cathedral, she would have to find a doorway to take shelter in. Wrapping her draggled cloak more tightly about her and bowing her head against the wind, she started determinedly down another street.

Suddenly, she heard the sounds of running feet and laughter ahead of her, and an instant later someone ran headlong into her. The impact knocked her down; for a few moments she lay winded on the hard cobbles. Slowly, she became aware of voices above her.

"I didn't even see her. Do you suppose she's hurt?"

"You shouldn't have been running, Geoffrey. Master told you not to."

"You're a big help," the first boy retorted; then he knelt down beside Alice. "Are you hurt, miss?"

Alice forced herself to sit up. "I don't think so."

"Let me help you up." He took her hands and pulled her to her feet. "It's lucky you weren't carrying eggs," he added with a smile. He frowned suddenly and peered closely at her. "Are you sure you're all right? You're kind of white."

She nodded. "But can — can you tell me how to get to the cathedral?"

The other boy nodded. "Sure. But what do you want there? Evensong is over."

"I was told I might find food and shelter."

"If you're hungry, just come along with us. It's the

least I can do after knocking you down. I'm Geoffrey Fisher and this is Nathaniel Denhem."

"Nate to friends," he put in.

"I'm Alice Tuckfield," she replied, then instantly wondered if that had been wise. Perhaps she should have made up a name, but her mind was slow with hunger and cold. They started down the street together. Fortunately, though the way was complicated, it wasn't far, for Alice's knees felt unpleasantly weak.

"Here we are," Geoffrey said as he led the way up some steps. He pushed open the heavy door, ushering Alice inside.

She found herself in a large kitchen with a red tile floor. An enormous fireplace took up most of one wall, and a large cauldron hung over the blaze. In the dim light from the candles and the fireplace, she could see several boys at work; two were washing dishes at the stone sink while another wiped down the tables and another plied a broom. Ropes of onions hung from the heavy beams, and the kitchen was filled with the smell of food. It made Alice realize how hungry and cold she was; she even felt a little dizzy. She took a deep breath to steady herself.

"Oh good," said Nate. "They're nearly done."

One of the boys at the sink tossed a dishtowel at them. "Some people have all the luck. We're just finishing. I don't know why Old Frost doesn't make me stay once in a while."

"Who's that with you?" asked another boy.

Geoffrey gave Alice a wink. "She's an old friend,

3

Randall — a cousin, in fact. I, er, ran into her on the street. She hasn't had any supper. Is there anything left?"

Randall looked from Alice's straight, dark hair to Geoffrey's wild, tawny mop and raised an eyebrow. "Cousin, Geoff? You should have stuck to friend. Orlando, find some food for the lass. There's a little stew left, and some bread. You'll want to wash, I expect," he added as he took Alice to a small, screened alcove where there was a washstand and basin, a pitcher of water, a cake of yellow soap and a hip bath in one corner. Though the water was icy, Alice gratefully washed her face and hands, drying them on the towel she found hanging on a hook.

When she had finished, Orlando handed her a large bowl of stew and a plate with bread and butter on it. "Go eat by the fire," he told her with a friendly smile. "You're as wet as a rat in a rain barrel."

She smiled wanly at him and took a seat in the large, battered armchair by the fireplace. With great effort, she made herself eat slowly. While she ate, the boys talked cheerfully, paying no particular attention to her. She was relieved; she didn't really feel she had the strength for conversation. When the food was gone, one of them took her dishes away to be washed. She pulled her knees up to her chin and, leaning against the arm of the chair, she fell asleep.

"Geoffrey," Randall said quietly, "what are we going to do with your, er, cousin?"

"I didn't really think," he confessed. "To tell you

4

the truth, Randall, I knocked her down. I thought a meal might make amends."

"But she's fast asleep in that chair. What are we going to do with her? Dame Agnes will have our skins — and hers too, like as not — if she's found here."

"There's the poorhouse," one suggested indifferently.

Orlando shook his head. "Over my dead body, Morris. They'd work her to death there."

"Well, she can't stay here," Morris said peevishly.

"Why not?" Geoffrey demanded, glaring at him. "There's that big empty cupboard on the third floor. She could sleep there. No one ever goes up there."

"That's a good idea, Geoffrey," Orlando said approvingly. "Then tomorrow we can decide what's the best thing to do."

"But what about her parents?" Randall asked. "Won't they be worried?"

"I don't think she has any," Nate put in. "She wanted to be directed to the cathedral — she was looking for food and shelter."

"Well then," Randall said, "someone had better take some sheets and blankets up to the third floor — and perhaps a rush mat, if one can be found. Now —"

"You can't be serious!" Morris cried. "She's a *girl!*"

"But we are serious," Orlando said sternly. "And if you know what's good for you, you won't go squeaking to the Dame — or anyone else."

At that moment, they heard heavy footsteps in the hallway and a woman's voice called out sharply, "What is taking you boys so long?"

"I guess I won't have to squeak, will I?" Morris said with a smirk.

Orlando didn't bother to respond. He looked around quickly. The back of the chair faced the doorway so that Alice, curled up, wasn't immediately visible. Orlando assumed a nonchalant pose, lounging against the arm of the chair, and whispered, "For God's sake, distract her."

Geoffrey erupted into action. He leapt up onto the table and struck a flamboyant dancer's attitude just as Dame Agnes walked in.

"Geoffrey Fisher! What *are* you doing up there?"

"I am teaching them the Highland Fling," he told her.

"Indeed? And the table is the place to do this?" she said sarcastically. "Get down this instant!" she snapped, then turned to the others. "I should think you'd have better things to do than to watch Geoffrey carry on! You older boys know you're supposed to set an example for the younger ones, but I turn my back and *this* is how you behave. I confess, Randall, I'm surprised at you; I thought you were more reliable."

Randall spread his hands helplessly. "But you know what Geoffrey's like, ma'am. There's no stopping him."

"Well, *I'll* stop him. Come here." She took hold of Geoffrey's ear. "And if you others don't behave a little better," she added warningly, "you'll get the same treatment." Then she marched Geoffrey out of the room.

"That was close," Randall said as soon as the Dame

was gone. "We'd better do this quickly. Timothy, get the bedding. Nate, you and Orlando take her upstairs and explain the plan. Morris, take that look off your face. I know you don't approve, but if you know what's good for you, you'll hold your tongue." He sounded very stern. Morris shrugged but did not answer.

Orlando reached down and shook Alice gently. "Here, wake up."

She blinked sleepily at him. "What is it?"

"You can't sleep down here," he told her. "We've fixed a place upstairs. Come on." He took her hand and helped her up. She was a little unsteady on her feet, so he held on to her elbow. Nate took a candle from the table by the door and, with a glance at Orlando, led them up two flights of narrow stairs to an empty room with an enormous cupboard set into one wall. Timothy was there already, arranging a rush mat, sheets, blankets and a fat pillow into a makeshift bed on one of the wide shelves.

"Now," Orlando said, "I'll try to explain quickly, because I can see you're as sleepy as a bear in winter. You can stay here for the night. Dame Agnes never comes up here, so it will be safe for you. In the morning, one of us will come up to get you once the Dame's gone out. We'll give you breakfast, then decide what to do. Have you got all that?"

She nodded.

"Remember," Nate admonished, "don't come down 'til one of us tells you it's clear."

She nodded again.

"We have to take the candles," Orlando said. "The Dame counts them. Goodnight."

"Goodnight."

As soon as they were gone, Alice stripped down to her shift. Her clothes were still damp, so she spread them out to dry as best she could in the dark. It was cold in the little garret, and she was shivering by the time she was done. She braced herself for the cold sheets and climbed into bed. To her surprise, she found that one of the boys (it must have been Timothy, she decided) had thought to put a warm brick in the make-shift bed. Gratefully, she snuggled into the warmth and closed her eyes. Almost immediately she was asleep.

CHAPTER TWO

Alice woke slowly the next morning. She hovered for quite some time in a sort of half wakefulness: warm and comfortable, forgetting the turmoil of the past few days. When she finally opened her eyes, she was disoriented by the dark closeness of her cupboard refuge; then she remembered.

She had been surprised when her father had told her they were going to Kirby Manor for a visit. Alice knew he had not been there since before her mother's death, but when she asked him about it, he would only say that he fancied some hunting. She had feared she would be bored, especially after he told her he would be busy with some guests from London, but she had found she liked the place. She got into the habit of escaping from her governess and roaming in the nearby woods, which were grandly referred to as "the park." That was how the nightmare had begun. She squeezed her eyes shut against the memory but could not stop it.

It had been the kind of afternoon that comes like a benediction at the very end of autumn. Alice had been unable to resist it. She had slipped away from the house and taken refuge in one of her favorite places: one of the huge beeches in the park. She sat high up, one arm hugging the great trunk of the tree, her cheek pressed against the smooth gray bark; a few tattered leaves clung stubbornly to the branches. All was still. There was no breeze. Not even a bird was stirring when suddenly, loud as shouting, she heard the sound of horses approaching. Two horses. She tried to make herself small, for though her father would understand her slipping out, if he were with someone, he would feel constrained to chastise her and send her back to Mistress Pelhame. She could see the riders now: her father, imposing on his large bay, and one of the two guests from London — Lord Crofton, she thought. They were still a short distance away when it happened. Her father checked in midword and, with a surprised little cry, slowly toppled from the saddle, an arrow quivering in his breast.

For several moments, Alice was too stunned even to scream. Lord Crofton dismounted quickly, though without apparent surprise, and examined his fallen host.

"Dead?" asked a voice nearly directly below Alice. She started, then held her breath, terrified.

"Dead," Crofton confirmed. "The Queen will be pleased, I do believe. A fine shot, Roderick."

The other man approached Lord Crofton, and Alice

recognized her father's other guest, Sir Roderick Donne. She covered her mouth with one hand.

"Thank you," he acknowledged, then looked down at Henry Tuckfield's still form. "Poachers' work, the sheriff will *undoubtedly* agree." His tone was mocking. "How tragic. Did anyone see you with him?"

"Do you take me for a fool?" Lord Crofton asked blandly. "Where's your horse?"

"Not far, not far," Sir Roderick replied calmly. "This way."

They walked beneath Alice's hiding place while she held perfectly still. She remained so for a long time after they had gone. Then she began to shiver uncontrollably. Shakily, she climbed down from the tree. She carefully avoided looking in her father's direction, while she decided what to do. Unbidden, a memory of her father surfaced: he was standing, dressed in all his finery, by the huge fireplace in the library of their London house; he was on his way to the Court of Queen Elizabeth. "Alice," he was saying, "promise me this: if ever you should find yourself in need, and myself unable to help you, seek out Lady Jenny at Chellisford Hall, in York. Promise."

Alice hesitated only long enough to decide she dared not risk a trip to the house. Mistress Pelhame would surely see her, and her chance would be lost. It was a good thing she had brought her cloak, for the night would be cold. Resolutely, she set off down the path to the main road. The sheriff must be told.

But long before she reached Kirbymoorside she realized it would be futile to go to the sheriff; the men had certainly bribed him. Besides, if Queen Elizabeth really would be pleased by the murder of her father, it was worse than foolish to try to raise a hue and cry. So Alice skirted the little town and went straight on toward York.

The journey had been nightmarish. She had spent the first night huddled in a ditch by the road and had woken, stiff and shivering, to a gray day, a biting wind and no hope of a meal. It began to rain before sunset, and the second night she barely slept at all. She trudged through the third day, drenched and miserable, only to find Chellisford Hall wasn't in York at all but well beyond it.

And then she had literally run into Geoffrey and Nate. She wondered why they were here, what this place was; she didn't think they'd told her last night, but she wasn't sure. She vaguely remembered that Orlando had said something about deciding what should be done. She lay on her back, puzzling over it, until she heard footsteps and the creak of the door opening.

"G'morning," Geoffrey called from the doorway. "Are you awake?"

"Yes, thank you, but I must have been rather sleepy last night, because I don't remember very much. Why do you all live here? Are you orphans?" Her voice caught slightly on the word: she was one now.

He laughed. "No! We're the boys in the cathedral choir. They keep us here so we're near at hand but out of trouble. Now, why don't you get dressed and come down to breakfast? Dame Agnes has gone out to do the marketing — she's usually gone an hour or two — and the younger boys are doing their lessons."

"Very well. Geoffrey, do you think — could I — do you suppose I could have a bath?"

"Orlando already thought of that. He's putting water on to heat. Hurry, now." She heard his footsteps start down the stairs.

As soon as he had gone she dressed quickly, then straightened her bedclothes. She shut the cupboard door firmly and went downstairs. The boys were busy with the washing up. When Randall saw her, he gestured to the table, where a large kettle sat on an iron trivet.

"Help yourself," he told her cheerfully.

Alice ladled porridge into a wooden bowl, added milk and honey, and began to eat. It tasted delicious. When she finished her first helping, she filled her bowl a second time, scraping the kettle clean, but she had barely started in on it when Orlando gave a sudden yelp of surprise.

"The Dame's coming back! Quick!" He swung a door open. "Into the closet — and take your porridge!"

Alice barely made it; Orlando shut her in the closet just as the heavy kitchen door scraped open.

"Well!" Dame Agnes said in surprise. "All of you slaving away like little saints? It isn't possible. You must be up to some mischief." Then she noticed the empty porridge kettle. "There was some porridge left over. What happened to it?"

There was an awkward pause, and in the broom closet Alice braced herself for what was surely coming. Then Geoffrey stepped into the breach.

"There didn't seem to be enough to bother saving, so I fed it to a stray puppy."

"A puppy? Geoffrey Fisher! You should know better!"

"But you don't understand, ma'am," Geoffrey said in his own defense. "It looked up at me with the biggest, saddest brown eyes that said, plain as words, 'I'm hungry, and tired, and cold. I haven't anyone to care for me nor anywhere to go. Please, please give me some breakfast.' So I fed it. I had to."

The Dame sighed. "Geoffrey, I swear you are enough to make a stone gargoyle weep. Now I suppose that wretched creature will be hanging about for weeks! You *mustn't* encourage it. We've been through all this before. I will not have a puppy in this house, and that is *final*." She looked around at them all sternly. "Now," she added more mildly, "where *is* my shopping list?" She bustled about until she found the list and again went out. Once the door was firmly shut behind her, Randall went to the closet and opened the door.

"You can come out now, Pup," he told her, grinning.

She emerged. "Don't call me that," she said, half laughing. "Geoffrey, whatever got into you to make you go on like that?"

"Sheer inspiration. I think I *shall* call you Pup. It suits you."

"Yes," Orlando agreed, laughing. "You have such big, puppy-brown eyes."

The others laughed, but Alice ignored it, sitting down at the table and primly continuing her breakfast. When she finished, she took her bowl and the empty kettle to Orlando at the sink and smiled a little shyly at him. "May I help?"

He grinned. "Pup, you shouldn't ask a question like that around loafers like us. You can dry." He handed her a dishtowel, and she set to work. After a few minutes, Orlando began to hum.

"I know that," Alice said, surprised. "It's a round."

"Do you sing?" he broke off to ask.

She nodded.

"I'll start, then, and you follow," he said, then launched into song. Alice joined in, and their two clear treble voices rang in the tiled kitchen.

There were low whistles when they finished. "She can *sing*, by heaven!" Randall exclaimed.

"Listen!" Geoffrey put in, his face alight with mischief. "I've just had the most wonderful idea! Let's make Pup into a choirboy and see how long she can sing in the choir before Master Frost notices!"

Nate caught the enthusiasm. "What a prank! I've a spare tunic that would fit, and we can cut her hair —"

"Now wait a minute!" Morris cut in. "You can't be serious! It was bad enough just for the night! I won't have some girl here."

"No?" Geoffrey demanded, clenching his fists and advancing on Morris. "Why not?"

Morris retreated a step. "But just *imagine* the trouble we'll get into when she's discovered! I don't want to risk a beating for some girl."

"You're an awful coward, Morris," Randall said with a pained expression. "Old Frost will never notice unless someone squeaks. But if it will make you feel better, *if* she's discovered, we'll let you pretend you didn't know about it. The younger boys won't know Pup is a girl, after all."

"That's right," Orlando agreed quickly. "And while you're imagining things, Morris Tedder, just think how you'd feel if you hadn't any home and were hungry and cold with winter coming on. You may be callous enough to toss Pup out into the street like an old marrow bone, but I'm not! I vote she stays!"

"Hear, hear," the others chorused.

"I don't want any part of it," Morris insisted. "You are all out of your minds."

"Come on, Morris," Timothy coaxed. "There's no harm in it."

"She's a *girl*, Timothy!" he retorted. "She doesn't belong here."

"Morris, we know how you feel, but the vote is against you," Orlando said softly but with menace. "There's no risk to you, but let me warn you, Morris: if you so much as think of telling on Pup, I'll make you sorrier than a horse at the knacker's."

"And I'll help him," Geoffrey added.

"But I don't want you to get in trouble for my sake," Alice protested.

"No chance of that, Pup," Timothy said. "Old Master Frost will never notice you so long as you don't sing flat."

"Now," Randall said. "Geoffrey, get the shears. Nate, you and Timothy go hunt up some clothing. Orlando, is the bath water hot yet? Good. Fill the hip bath so Pup can have her bath after I've cut her hair. Who's got a comb? Ready, Pup?"

Randall made short, somewhat ragged work of her hair, then sent her off to the screened alcove to bathe, admonishing her to hurry since they had a rehearsal that morning. She bathed quickly, then dressed in the clothes Nate and Timothy had found: a pair of brown leggings only a little too large, a sturdy linen shirt, a heavy wool tunic, much mended, and a well-worn pair of soft leather shoes that were slightly too tight. She felt oddly unencumbered without her long skirt, but she decided it would be more comfortable once she got used to it. She folded up her old clothing and emerged from the alcove. Geoffrey clapped her on the back, then handed her a fleece-lined jacket.

"Why, you look just like one of us. All you need is a halo. Run upstairs and put your old stuff away — but hurry! We need to get there early enough to introduce you to the other boys."

"But aren't there men in the choir?" she asked as a nagging question surfaced. "Won't they notice an extra treble?"

"Even if they do notice you (which isn't very likely), they won't make any comment," Orlando reassured her.

"Why should they? Master Frost doesn't consult them every time he adds a voice. Now, relax."

"But watch out for Master Kenton," Timothy put in unexpectedly. "He's the accompanist. He doesn't like us boys, but as long as you stay well out of his way, he won't bother you."

Alice nodded and hurried to put her things away. When she returned, they went out into the brisk, gray day. In the light it was easier for Alice to get a sense of where they were, though the narrow lanes and streets were still confusing. They wound their way through the Shambles until they came out on a slightly wider street — Lop Lane, she read on a battered sign. Then Lop Lane opened onto an even wider street with quite a lot of traffic on it. The boys threaded their way around carriages and wagons, pedestrians and riders, until they came to an opening on the left-hand side. They went into a narrow alley with a pair of heavy iron gates — standing open now — at the end of it.

"Minster gates," Geoffrey told Alice over his shoulder. When they passed through, they were suddenly in the cathedral close. Yorkminster towered over them. It was a magnificent building, with three majestic square towers rising about it. Alice caught her breath and stopped.

Orlando tugged at her sleeve. "It *is* impressive," he murmured, "but we must hurry. You can come back later, you know."

Alice nodded and they trotted after the others. They went along the south side of the building, then around the east end. Instead of going into the cathedral, as Alice had expected, they turned up a narrow street called Vicar Lane. They passed a large stone building on the left with ST. WILLIAM'S COLLEGE carved above the door, then went up the steps of the house two doors past it. A wooden plaque by the door read ST. PETER'S CHOIR SCHOOL.

Once inside, they went down a narrow corridor toward an open door. When they reached the room at the end of the corridor, Alice found herself bustled into place on one of the hard benches set up for the singers. There was an enormous fireplace on one wall, with a fire laid but not lit. Alice wished it *were* lit, for the room wasn't any too warm. There was a noisy crowd of younger boys milling about; they looked at Alice curiously.

"Listen!" Geoffrey commanded. The babble was instantly stilled. He lowered his voice. "This is Pup. He's going to sing with us. We thought it would be a grand prank to see how long it takes old Frost to notice him. What do you think?"

There were a few cheers and some delighted laughter.

Geoffrey nodded emphatically. "I knew you'd all be game."

The boys crowded around Alice and pelted her with names. She laughed and held up one hand. "It will take me a while to sort all of you out."

Orlando came over to her. "You'd better sit down before the men start arriving. No sense in standing out in a crowd, if you know what I mean."

Alice took his point and sat down in the second row between Geoffrey and Orlando. Very soon, the men began to arrive. They took no notice of the boys, simply seating themselves and continuing their quiet conversations. Alice tried to still the butterflies in her stomach; she was just beginning to sneak covert glances at the other singers when a man came in carrying a large sheaf of music.

"That's old Frost," Geoffrey told her.

Alice raised her eyebrows in amazement, for he wasn't at all what she had expected. From the boys' references to "old" Frost, she had pictured a frail, white-haired gentleman with a dreamy, somewhat vague expression. Master Frost was none of those things. His hair was grizzled, and there were streaks of silver in his neat beard, but it did not make him look old; nothing could have, for there was great energy in his movement and an infectious enthusiasm in his brown eyes. Alice fought the urge to flee: the whole thing had been a stupid idea and he would see through it in an instant! She gripped her hands together in her lap. The boys had *said* he wouldn't notice her, she insisted to herself; they must have had reason to believe it. She took a deep breath and waited.

Master Frost handed the sheaf of music to a man in the front row with some instructions. Though Alice couldn't hear the words, she felt the resonance of his deep voice in the air. A moment later, sheets of music were being passed to her by a suddenly anxious-looking Orlando.

"I say, Pup," he whispered, "you can read music, can't you? In all the excitement we forgot to ask." At her nod, his brow lightened. "That's lucky. It would have been frightfully awkward if you couldn't."

"Let's stand up," said Master Frost from his podium. "Take a good stretch, get all the kinks out. Now, on a hee-heh-ha-ho-hoo..." The accompanist struck a chord on the virginal (Alice hadn't even noticed it, and the unexpected timbre nearly made her jump), and the rehearsal began.

It didn't take Alice long to discover why the boys thought Master Frost would never notice her; he was far too wrapped up in the music, in the sound of the whole choir, to notice one small, unfamiliar face. But all the same, she sang rather timidly.

It was a good choir, she decided, with a good accompanist. Master Kenton, at least, was much as she had imagined him: a thin, rather grim-faced man, with graying hair and a faintly sarcastic expression except in his eyes. They were pale gray and piercing, but there was a hint of distance in them, as if he were listening to something very far away. The look in his eyes seemed familiar to Alice; she realized, with a tightness in her throat, that her father had often looked like that, with his hands on the keyboard and his thoughts far away.

When the rehearsal was over, the boys hurried back toward the dormitory for their noon meal. "After lunch," Geoffrey told her as they walked, "we have lessons. You won't have to go — lucky you — so perhaps you can explore the cathedral. There's plenty to see.

There are stairways that go clear up to the top of the towers — the view from up there is great. And there's the crypt — that's pretty wonderful, too — but you'd need the key."

"But won't people think it odd for a choirboy to be wandering about when he ought to be in his lessons?"

"I don't think anyone will notice, but even if they do, you don't have CHOIRBOY etched on your forehead. Just look innocent."

"But what about lunch?" she asked as they neared the door.

"You're full of worries, Pup," he told her patiently. "Just loiter outside. I'll bring you something."

True to his word, Geoffrey returned in a short while carrying half a loaf of bread and a generous hunk of cheese wrapped in a linen napkin. While Alice ate, Geoffrey perched on a stone railing and outlined the plan for the afternoon and evening.

"We're all at our lessons until four, then at half past we congregate for a brief rehearsal before Evensong. I'll meet you by the main door a little after four — the cathedral bell tolls the hours, you know — and I'll find you a cassock and surplice. Then, after the service, we all go to dinner. You'll have to wait outside while we eat, but once the younger boys go upstairs and we start the cleanup, someone will come and get you. Is that clear?"

"I'm to meet you by the main door at four o'clock," she replied obediently.

"Right you are. Now, I must fly. 'Til later."

Alice finished as much of the bread and cheese as she wanted, wrapped the remainder up again in the napkin, and tucked it into a pocket in her jacket. Then she set off for the cathedral. Geoffrey had been right about no one noticing her. She was able to wander as she pleased, reading inscriptions beneath statues and on stone or bronze plaques on the wall and gazing in awe at the beautiful windows. When she was poking about into nooks and crannies, she found a spiral staircase tucked into the wall like a sentry box. She started up it.

It was a long climb. Before Alice reached the top, she was almost sorry she had started, but she kept on. Geoffrey had said the view was good. At last she reached the top. She was in a little round room that gave on a walk running behind the crenelations on top of the lanthorn tower. Alice ran to the wall in delight. Beneath her, York was spread out like an old patchwork. She could see the crowded rooftops of the Shambles and the old Roman walls running through the city. She walked around the battlements, trying to pick out landmarks from the unfamiliar vantage point. She recognized Monk Gate and the two rivers, the Ouse and the Foss; she *thought* she could pick out St. Andrewgate and the Horsefair, but she wasn't sure. She looked for Chellisford Hall in the gray and brown lands beyond the city, but since she wasn't sure which direction to look, she didn't think she'd found it. After she tired of the view, she took out the bread she had saved from lunch and spent a few minutes trying to coax some of the pigeons to eat from her hand. When she got cold, she went back down.

Once back on the ground, she slipped into the choir and sat down in the choir stalls. There was such peace in the cathedral; she found it reassuring and comforting, especially after the hectic confusion and anxieties of the morning. She found herself wondering whether it would work, this rather harebrained scheme of Geoffrey's, and she realized that she wanted it to — very much — and for more reason than the simple fear of being again out in the cold. She liked the boys, and the choir, too; but for a fleeting moment she wondered if Orlando and Geoffrey's threats would really keep Morris, or anyone else, from telling on her.

"Oh well," she told herself, "I can always go to Chellisford Hall." But she dreaded being discovered and sent away; she realized how much she wanted to stay with these new friends.

"A Tuckfield must land on his feet." She heard her father's voice in her mind, and the grief she had shut away broke loose. She bowed her head, covering her face with her hands while silent tears welled between her fingers.

CHAPTER THREE

How long she sat there Alice wasn't sure, but gradually she became aware of voices behind her. She knew she shouldn't eavesdrop, but there was a furtive air about them that piqued her curiosity. She crouched down in the choir stall, trying to be inconspicuous, and strained her ears to hear.

". . . don't know what to do . . . damned inconvenient . . . peasants are agog with it."

"Peasants are peasants." The second voice was more distinct and had a markedly affected accent. "You needn't bother about them. He kept the brat rather shut away. You ought to be able to make something out of that."

"You mean put it about that she is mad? But the governess . . ."

The other sighed. "Buy her silence — or her corroboration," he said in a bored tone. "Why must I think of everything?"

"What about when she turns up? And where can she be?"

"As to that, I've a fair idea. Hal was thick as thieves with Lady Jenny in the old days. The child will turn up at Chellisford Hall within the week."

Alice stifled a gasp. They were talking about *her!*

"How can you speak so calmly —" His voice rose, but the other hushed him.

"Relax. Lady Jenny is in France, and I'm having a close watch kept on Chellisford Hall. I'll have the brat as soon as she surfaces."

"And then?"

"I'll send you word. You or Roderick can dispose of her as you see fit. I'll leave that matter in your hands."

There were rustlings as the men rose. "I just hope you know what you're doing, Dunstan. What if she doesn't surface?"

"She will. She hasn't any money, and she must eat."

Alice, cowering in the shadows, listened to their footsteps as they passed her and continued toward the front of the cathedral. She didn't dare to move, not even to steal a look at them. As their footsteps faded, she began to tremble. Lady Jenny was in France. Chellisford Hall was being watched. *Now* what would she do when she was discovered and sent away from the cathedral?

"Then I mustn't be discovered — it's that simple,"

she told herself resolutely, trying to muster her courage. After a time, the cathedral bell tolled four. She shook off her fear as best she could and went to the front door to meet Geoffrey.

"Well, Pup," he greeted her. "Did you enjoy your afternoon?"

She nodded. While Geoffrey led her up a flight of stairs to the organ loft, she told him about feeding the pigeons on top of the tower. The organ was built into the choir screen, an ornately carved wooden structure that separated the choir from the nave. From the organ loft, Alice had a clear view of the choir and the high altar or, if she faced the other way, of the lanthorn tower and the nave. Again, she felt overwhelming awe at the sheer size and magnificence of the cathedral. She stood gazing up at the inside of the lanthorn tower, its square bulk filled with the reddish late afternoon light, while Geoffrey rummaged in a closet. After a few minutes, he produced a black cassock and held it up to Alice's shoulder.

"That ought to do," he said. A moment's further search uncovered a white surplice. "Here you are." He made her a mock-serious bow. "Your raiment, sir chorister."

She took the things with a slightly wan smile, then turned to examine the organ. It was an imposing instrument, with rank upon rank of enormous silver pipes. There were four keyboards, a pedal board, and countless ivory knobs with odd names on them in elegant script. She timidly reached out and depressed a key. Nothing happened. Geoffrey laughed at her chagrin.

"First of all, you need someone to pump it." He took her around in back of the ranks of pipes and showed her the enormous bellows. "And then you need to pull out one of the stops — those are the knob things. They make the air go through different pipes. But come on. We have to go downstairs. We will be rehearsing in the cathedral, but someone would be sure to think it odd if I were *early*."

As they started down the stairs, puzzlement gathered on Alice's face. "Geoffrey, are the boys just at Evensong? Doesn't Master Frost have a full choir at Matins, too?"

"Of course. Matins and Evensong every day. Eucharist on Sunday, and special services on saints' days. We go to Matins first thing, while the Dame cooks our breakfast."

"Someone will have to get me up pretty early if I'm going to be at Matins and not run into the Dame."

Geoffrey nodded. "We thought of that. Orlando's always up early. He'll see you're up in time." He grinned at her as he hurried her across the transept and out through the enormous south doors. "Don't worry so, Pup. It will age you."

She grinned back. "You're such a harebrain, Geoffrey. I need to be certain *someone's* thought of these things."

Once outside, they met a crowd of the other boys who

were coming from the school building. Randall waved at them, and they joined him.

"I see Geoffrey found you something to wear," he remarked as they went back inside.

Alice nodded, but before she could reply, Orlando bounced up to them, hastily buttoning his cassock.

"Hi, Pup. You can sit with me, can't you?" Without waiting for her reply, he pulled his surplice over his head and thrust his arms into the wide sleeves. Alice put her cassock and surplice on while the others ran up to the organ loft to get theirs; then they went into the choir and took their seats in the choir stalls. Alice was between Orlando and Geoffrey again, with Randall sitting in the next row forward. She felt a quiver of apprehension in her stomach, but she sat quietly while they waited for Master Frost.

The rehearsal and the service went without a major hitch, though there was a brief moment of anxiety near the beginning of the service when Alice almost forgot to stand up. She had been lost in the intricate organ music Master Kenton had played for a prelude. Orlando and Geoffrey had managed to get her to her feet in time so that no harm was done, but for the rest of the service Alice felt awkward. When it was over, the boys and Alice hung up their cassocks and surplices. Alice and Orlando loitered while the others filed out, and they followed them from a distance. When they reached the dormitory, Orlando turned to her. "You're a good sport, Pup. It shouldn't be too long."

She managed a smile as she watched him disappear into the kitchen, then she sat down on the step and huddled into her jacket. Tomorrow, after the evening service she would stay in the cathedral, where it was at least a little warmer, but today she hadn't been altogether certain she could find her way back by herself. It might be cold, but at least she knew she would have supper and a roof over her head.

While she sat waiting, Alice couldn't help thinking how different this was from what she was used to. She had never had to worry, before, about what she would eat or where she would sleep. She had spent her life hedged about by servants and governesses, tutored and sheltered. Though she had grown up in London, York seemed a bigger place to her; for the first time in her life, she was on her own. Alice felt the lump in her throat again. She missed them all — her father, their housekeeper Anne, her music tutor Master Hunnis, even her governess. Sometimes they had fussed over her too much, especially Anne, but now she would have welcomed their warmhearted scolding. She bit her lip, trying hard not to cry.

"Psst!" Nate's voice shook her out of her reflections. "It's all clear, Pup."

She suddenly realized how cold she was. Without waiting to be told twice she slipped inside, took the plate of roast chicken and baked potato that had been laid out for her, and curled up in the armchair by the fire.

"Hey!" Geoffrey said teasingly. "No puppies on the furniture."

She opened her eyes wide and looked up at him. "I thought you couldn't resist my pleading brown eyes."

The others laughed and Geoffrey joined in. "Hurry up and finish so you can help. We need to be done before Dame Agnes gets suspicious."

Soon the washing up was finished and they all got ready to go up. Geoffrey walked Alice to her room.

"G'night, Pup," he said, then paused on his way out the door. "You don't really mind being called Pup, do you? Because if you do, I can try to make the others stop."

She smiled. "I really don't mind, Geoffrey. Goodnight."

During the next few days, Alice settled into the routine. She rose early each morning and met the boys at Matins. The rest of the morning was spent in rehearsal, and during the afternoon she explored either the cathedral or the town. One day, she went to see the Archbishop's Palace — it was really just an especially grand house, she decided, and not a palace at all — and on another she investigated the bustling marketplace, which was almost as exciting as a fair. On one particularly nasty afternoon, she climbed up to the bell tower. She was fascinated by the enormous bronze bells and found it almost impossible to resist pulling the ropes that would set them swinging. She discovered a stairway that led up to a narrow passage behind the open arches that looked down into the church (it was called the triforium, Randall told her), and she had fun pretending to be a spy and sneaking from arch to arch as she watched the people in the nave.

During rehearsal one morning, Master Frost passed out an anthem that he said they would use on Sunday.

"Most of you know this, I think," he told them, "but we'll run through it once, just to be sure."

"Know it indeed," Geoffrey whispered to Pup as he handed her a copy. "Master Kenton made me and Nate copy it fifteen times each for being rude in class."

She smiled and took the music, but as she looked down at it she froze. "Rejoice, O My Soul" she read, "a verse anthem in five parts by Sir Henry Tuckfield." A vivid memory surfaced. Her father had been playing the virginal in the music room of their house in London. Master William Hunnis, the choirmaster of the Chapel Royal, had looked over his shoulder, humming along. Alice had sat unnoticed, watching them both. When he had finished, her father had looked back at his friend.

"Well? What do you think? Can you use it?"

Master Hunnis had smiled his rare smile. "It's lovely, Hal. Of course I will."

"That's good, then," he had said, sweeping up the music and pushing it into Master Hunnis's hands. "Just put in a good word with Her Majesty for me."

"You don't need my good words, Hal," Master Hunnis had said almost sharply. "Just learn to govern that cursed unruly tongue of yours once in a while!"

Alice's father had laughed. "Don't scold me, William; I do my best. I —" He had broken off when he caught sight of Alice. He had held out his hands to her, smiling as she came to him. "Alice! I didn't see you there. Don't you get bored listening to two old men like us?"

She had shaken her head. "I like to," she had replied seriously.

He had laughed, hugged her. "Alice, you're a treasure. Run along and do your lessons, and I'll take you into town with me later."

Geoffrey nudged her sharply. "Pup!" he whispered. "Are you all right?"

She looked up at him, her lips pressed together. She could feel the tears brimming in her eyes. She nodded once, swallowing hard, and bent her head, willing herself not to cry. Then Master Kenton began to play and one of the tenors sang the solo verse. Alice managed to move her mouth in time with the others when the choir came in, but she knew no sound could emerge around the terrible lump in her throat.

After the rehearsal, Geoffrey held her back a ways from the others. "Are you really all right, Pup?" he asked her.

"Yes," she assured him. "I guess breakfast didn't entirely agree with me. I felt a little strange during rehearsal, but I'm fine now."

He looked at her skeptically, then a little awkwardly put his arm around her shoulders. "Look, Pup, if there's anything I can do, anything at all . . ."

She shook her head. "I told you, I'm fine now." But she could hear a faint tremor in her voice.

"I know. But I mean —"

"I know what you mean," she interrupted quietly, smiling wanly at him. "And I'm glad you're my friend, Geoffrey."

He slapped her gently on the back. "Come on, then."

Together, they went off through the cathedral close toward the Dame's.

On Sunday morning, Alice had been up and dressed for a while when Geoffrey came in looking anxious. "Pup, we have a problem," he told her. "Orlando overslept. We meant to have you up and out before breakfast. The Dame doesn't go out on Sundays. Sometimes she goes back to her own rooms while we do washing up, but this morning she's settled herself in front of the fire and it doesn't look as though she'll *ever* shift."

"Can I go out the front way?"

"You'd never get the door open without her hearing. Once it gets cold, we don't use that door much, and she bolts it shut. But this is what we're going to try: You come down to the landing below the second floor and wait. Nate will go into the parlor and knock something over with a crash. The Dame, we hope, will jump up and run out to see what happened. When she goes

34

past the foot of the stairs, you come down and flit out. Orlando will have the door open for you. Wait for us by the south door of the cathedral."

"Now wait a minute, Geoffrey. Why do we have to do this? Can't I just forget about the service and stay here?"

He shook his head. "It's too dangerous. For one thing, the Dame's downstairs, and for another, we'd really be in the stew if someone asked us where you were in front of old Frost. I can almost hear him: 'What new boy? I don't think I auditioned a new boy this week.' You *have* to be there."

"Very well. But I still have some questions. What about the younger boys? You didn't tell them I was staying here. What are they going to think?"

"Don't worry about *them*. The Dame shooed them all outside a little while ago, said they were driving her mad."

"That's a relief, I suppose. Still, can't we do this some other way? It seems to me that Nate's very likely to get a beating for his part in this."

Geoffrey shrugged. "Nate's really good at turning the Dame up sweet. I expect he'll wriggle out of it. Besides, Pup, he did volunteer. Now, there isn't time for any more argument. Come on."

She followed Geoffrey downstairs and waited on the landing while he went into the kitchen. Nate, who was lurking just outside the door, gave her a cheery wave and a conspiratorial wink. Then he disappeared down the hall. A moment later there came a loud crash, the unmistakable sound of breaking glass. Alice bit her lips together.

"What was that?" The Dame's voice came shrilly from the kitchen.

"I'll go see." That was Morris! He was trying to ruin it. He smirked in Alice's direction before he turned toward the parlor. For a moment all was quiet, then there came a couple of heavy thumps and a loud cry.

"What is going on?" the Dame demanded, her voice becoming louder as she approached the door. As she emerged and followed the two boys into the parlor, Alice shot down the stairs, darted into the kitchen, and went straight out the door. Orlando shut it behind her an instant before Dame Agnes returned, dragging each boy by the ear.

"Orlando, make a cold compress for Morris's eye. Randall, get some rags and help me stop this nosebleed. Geoffrey, go sweep up the remains" — she glared reproachfully at Nate — "of my favorite vase. Now Morris, why were you brawling with Nate in this shocking manner?"

"He started it!" Nate put in hotly. "He called me a clumsy —"

"I asked Morris."

"I didn't say a thing! As soon as I walked into the room, he jumped on me."

The Dame regarded him sternly. "Nate is usually a very steady boy. Would he really hit you for no reason? Are you sure you didn't say anything?"

"He had a reason, but it wasn't anything I said."

Randall made a quick, emphatic gesture to Timothy, who was hovering anxiously by the door. The boy slipped out.

"Would you care to explain this reason?" she pursued grimly.

"He called me a clumsy ox, and whatever he says now, he's just trying to wriggle out of it!" Nate cried angrily.

"I am speaking to Morris," she said with awful emphasis. "Well?"

Morris glared about the room with his one good eye. "They're hiding a girl on the third floor. Nate broke the vase on purpose so you'd leave the kitchen and she could get out. He hit me because I was trying to spoil it."

There was a stunned silence. "A girl?" Orlando said incredulously. "A *girl?*"

Randall looked down at Morris, shaking his head pityingly. "You really *will* say anything to get out of a beating, but this is farfetched, even for you."

"It's *true* and you know it!" Morris was almost choking with indignation.

"Morris," Orlando said patiently, "if you want to be believed you must either tell the truth or a better lie. Why on *earth* would we hide a girl? Now, if you'd said a *puppy* maybe Dame Agnes would believe you."

"Now, Morris —" the Dame began, but he interrupted her.

"There's a simple way to prove what I say! All her

stuff is in the third-floor cupboard: clothes, blankets, bedding. Come on! I'll show you."

"Morris," Randall said wonderingly, then turned to the Dame. "I don't understand . . . He must be ill. Why else would he persist in this foolish lie?"

Morris stamped his foot, speechless with rage.

Dame Agnes looked from Randall to Morris, then shook her head. "I think we'd better get to the bottom of this," she said grimly. "Morris, you show me what you're talking about. Randall, you and Orlando come too." She marched the three boys up the stairs. Morris yanked open the cupboard and his jaw dropped. It was empty.

"Well!" Dame Agnes exclaimed. "So you've had your little joke, Morris."

"They must have moved the things," he persisted.

"Who?" she retorted with scorn. "Orlando? Has he discovered how to be in two places at once?"

"Geoffrey —"

"Geoffrey was out of the room before this absurd discussion even began. This has gone far enough! I can't imagine what you hoped to gain by this, but let me warn you: if I ever hear one more word from you on the subject, I'll give you a thrashing you'll never forget. As it is, you shall miss your supper tonight."

Morris drew breath to protest but thought better of it at the look the Dame gave him. His shoulders slumped in defeat.

"And," Dame Agnes added, "you shall apologize to Nate for calling him a clumsy ox."

"Yes, ma'am," he replied meekly and followed her down the stairs.

Randall and Orlando met each other's eyes, and Orlando made fanning motions with his hand before they followed the others downstairs.

When the boys met Alice at the cathedral a little later, she greeted them with an anxious query. "You didn't get a beating, Nate?"

A slow grin spread over his face. "No, I didn't. And I blacked one of that snake Morris's eyes for him, too."

She looked mystified.

"We'll tell you the whole tale after the service," Geoffrey assured her. "And by the way, Pup, don't you think you ought to get rid of those girl's things? It's a bit risky to leave them lying about."

"Oh!" Remorse struck her. "Oh, I didn't think. I'll get rid of them just as soon as I can."

Geoffrey's smile turned a little rueful. "No need. Timothy and I already did."

CHAPTER FOUR

In the excitement of outwitting the Dame, Alice hadn't had a chance to think about the service — her first Sunday service! — or to realize how nervous she was; even during rehearsals her mind had been on the music. But now, as she and the others waited by the south door for the prelude to end, her stomach felt jumpy. There seemed to be an awful lot of people in the cathedral; there were also a fair number of people who were not in the choir but were obviously part of the service. One man held a strange object that looked like a metal egg hanging on a chain; looking more closely, she saw the holes in its top half. It was called a thurible, she remembered; it held incense. Another man carried a large gold cross on a long pole. The priests wore richly embroidered vestments over their white albs. She noticed that four choirboys, including Timothy and Geoffrey, each held a large candle in a brass holder. Geoffrey grimaced at her and came over.

"I have to be an acolyte today — I forgot it was my turn. Go with Orlando. He'll keep an eye on you."

"That's right," Orlando agreed. "I'll keep you in step. But I think old Kenton is winding up. We'd better get ready."

A moment later the organ sounded the final cadence and Master Frost, seeming to materialize out of nowhere, gave the choir the signal to begin the introit. The music floated around Alice and filled the cathedral, but she was too nervous to enjoy it. The introit ended, the last note shimmering into silence; then the organ began the hymn. The procession lined up quickly: first the man with the thurible — he swung it, and the sweet-smelling smoke came out of the holes — then the man with the cross, then the four choirboys with candles, walking two by two; the rest of the choirboys fell into line, Alice beside Orlando and behind Randall and Nate. They marched across the transept, down the north aisle, across the back, then straight up the center of the nave. It felt like an immense distance to Alice, as she imagined countless critical eyes upon her. When they reached the front of the choir the line split, each half going to the choir stalls on their side of the cathedral.

"That's the worst of it," Randall whispered between verses, "the procession."

Alice managed a weak smile. The hymn finished and they sang the Kyrie, and everything went smoothly until it came time for communion. They finished singing the Agnus Dei and lined up in front of the altar.

41

After Alice knelt down, the priest placed the bread on her tongue, murmuring the ritual words; a moment later, she received the wine but nearly choked. For the voice that intoned "The blood of our Lord Jesus Christ which was shed for thee, preserve thy body and soul unto everlasting life" was familiar: it was the affected voice of one of the men she had overheard talking so calmly of disposing of her. She felt sick. It should have occurred to her to wonder why those men had met in the cathedral to discuss their business, but that one of them was a priest! It was unthinkable; and it made her position doubly dangerous, for now if she were discovered . . . She wrenched her mind away from the thought and forced herself to behave normally as she followed the others back to her seat.

For the rest of the service, Alice was all but useless. She managed to stand, sit, and kneel in the right places and at least to mouth along when the others sang, but her mind was elsewhere, working furiously. It wasn't until the middle of the recessional hymn that she realized that even if she was discovered as a girl, the priest would have no way of knowing that she was in fact Alice Tuckfield. The thought cheered her only a little, for he would be bound to suspect. But perhaps his uncertainty would give her time to escape.

Finally, the service was over and they were outside in the pale sunlight.

"You made it through," Orlando whispered with a smile, but Randall looked concerned.

"Are you all right, Pup? You don't look very well."

"I'll be fine in a minute. All that smoke was beginning to make me feel queasy. Why do they burn it?" she asked, hoping to distract him.

"It's supposed to purify things," he told her ruefully. "You'll get used to it, Pup, no fear."

"What are we loitering for?" Geoffrey demanded. "Let's go to dinner."

"What about me?" Alice asked.

"You can come. On Sundays," Orlando added, adopting a pompous manner and an affected accent that reminded Alice strongly of the conspirator-priest, "the choristers dine in the Bedern with the vicars-choral except for one Sunday a month, when the entire choir is invited to dine with the Dean or the Sub-Dean. If I mistake not, today we dine with the Sub-Dean, the worthy Father Cooper."

"But surely I'll be noticed," she protested.

"In all that crowd?" Geoffrey said. "Not likely."

"Besides, if anyone *has* noticed you, it will be thought odd if you aren't there," Randall assured her. "Choirboys are traditionally hungry, and they feed us well. Don't worry, Pup. A dinner is much easier than a service."

They started up Precentors Lane, toward the Sub-Dean's residence.

"Which one is Father Cooper? Were you mimicking him, Orlando?" Alice asked, fearing his answer. If the conspirator *was* the Sub-Dean . . . She suppressed a shudder.

Orlando grinned. "Yes. He's the one who served the

wine. He's very stuffy. We all make fun of him. Just wait 'til you hear one of his sermons."

Alice's heart sank, but she managed to maintain a light tone. "That bad, eh?"

"He is," Randall announced ponderously, "oppressively eloquent."

"Long-winded," Geoffrey translated with a smile.

"Hallo there, scamps." A new voice greeted them cheerfully, and they were joined by one of the men. He turned to Alice and shook her hand. "You're new, aren't you? It's just like Master Frost to forget to introduce you. I'm Emery Morcocke."

"I'm Pup."

"Pup?" He grinned accusingly at Geoffrey. "Your idea, imp?"

Geoffrey affected innocence and Emery turned to Alice. "Do you mind their teasing much?"

She shook her head. "You know, I've never had a nickname before, nor friends my own age." The instant she said it she regretted it, for Emery looked at her curiously.

"Oh? Where are you from?"

"I grew up in London," she replied, fighting down panic and resolving to stay as close to the truth as possible. "An only child. I didn't meet any boys my own age."

"And how did you end up in York?" Emery pursued.

"It was plague," she replied simply and sadly. "My father died of it. I came here because my mother was born in York, but all her family is gone away or dead."

44

"London to York? That's a long trip for a boy your age. How did you manage?"

"I traveled with a man who knew my father. A merchant in woolens."

"I see." Emery smiled comfortingly at her. "And your mother? Did she die of the plague as well?"

"No. She died when I was very small. I don't remember her." Alice noticed, then, that the boys had been listening intently to her tale, and she realized, suddenly, how little they knew of her—or she of them. But there was no more time for speculation, for they had arrived at a great stone house and were mounting the front steps to the massive oak door. Geoffrey gave her an encouraging wink.

Before they even had a chance to knock, the door was flung open by Father Cooper himself. He greeted them jovially, smiling broadly.

"Come in, come in, my good choristers," he said heartily. "There's a good fire in the parlor, and as soon as everyone is here, we'll begin. I trust you brought your appetites, heh-heh-heh." He ushered them into the parlor, then went back to the door to greet the next group of singers.

"'Come in, come in,'" Geoffrey whispered in perfect mimicry as the door shut behind the priest. "Ugh."

Emery shook a reproving finger at him. "Don't make mock of your elders, my boy—especially when they are feeding you. One thing I will say for Father Cooper is that he sets a lavish table."

"He must," Alice murmured, thinking of his paunch.

45

"Oh-ho, a wit!" Emery laughed. "But it's clear you've never heard him pray. That thing the worthy Father wears about his waist is not a stomach at all — it's a *bellows*."

Randall and Geoffrey shook reproving fingers at the young man. " 'Don't make mock of your elders — especially when they are feeding you,' " Geoffrey quoted, but their banter was cut off abruptly when Father Cooper returned at the head of a large group of choristers.

"Here they are, the last of the lambs to the fold," the priest said, leading the entire group through yet another door into what was clearly the dining room. There were several large tables, one laden with food and piles of dishes and silverware and the others covered with linen tablecloths and set with pewter pitchers and crystal decanters. "Now," he went on, "let us bow our heads in prayer . . ."

The blessing was a long one. Alice's mind quickly shut out the rolling phrases as she concentrated instead on identifying the many tantalizing aromas. Roast beef, certainly, she decided, fish, and — was it venison? "Amen," she murmured with the others, then joined the eager, jostling line.

She was delighted with the variety of dishes: fish stew, a roast of beef, game pies, a casserole of chicken, a blood pudding (which she didn't sample), several kinds of bread, including delicate little dinner rolls, three sorts of vegetables (glazed carrots, baked squash and mashed turnip) and a choice of milk, wine or ale.

"I'll never be able to fit everything on my plate," she whispered to Geoffrey.

Geoffrey grinned at her. "Just take what you can carry — you can come back for more. But don't forget dessert."

"Dessert?"

He nodded. "Two or three kinds of pie and a cake or two, generally. Father Cooper doesn't do things by half."

"I guess not," she agreed as she helped herself to turnip and looked about. "Where shall we sit?"

"Nate's saved some places for us," Orlando volunteered. "See him wave?"

A few moments later they were settled on the long benches at Nate's table. "This beats scraps and leftovers, doesn't it, Pup?" he asked through a mouthful. "Eat up, though. It's just weak gruel and dry bread at the Dame's tonight. She always counts on our stuffing ourselves Sunday noon."

"What happens this afternoon?" she asked. "You don't have lessons, do you?"

"No, but most of us have some studying to do," Nate said glumly.

"But isn't there an evening service?" she persisted.

"No, not for us. But listen, Pup," Geoffrey said, "I haven't much that needs doing — just some harmony exercises for old Sourface Kenton, but then, he's never pleased with me anyway. We can cut out and visit my

47

gram. She's always glad to see me — and a friend — and she might even be able to scare up a few extra shirts and so forth for you."

"But won't you get into trouble?"

"Pup," he said with patience, "haven't you learned yet? I am always in trouble. Besides, you deserve a treat, the way you've sailed through this week. The worst is over now, you know."

The rest of the meal went quickly, the boys and Alice in high spirits. After they'd finished dessert, the entire gathering rose and thanked their host in unison (a ritual, Randall had explained, dating from the founding of the choir), then took their leave. They would all have felt less carefree if they had caught the long, somewhat questioning look Master Frost directed at Alice.

It was well after supper when Geoffrey and Alice returned to Dame Agnes's. The washing up was over, and though the younger boys had gone up to bed, Orlando, Randall and Nate were sprawled on the hearth rug in the kitchen, struggling over some books.

"Did you have a nice time?" Randall asked.

"Oh, yes," Alice replied. "She's a dear. She baked gingerbread for us and told us stories about the mischief Geoffrey's mother got into when she was little. And look," she added, holding out a bundle of clothing. "Two wool tunics, three good shirts, another pair of leggings and this" — she held out the prize of the

collection, a long-sleeved tunic lined with fleece —
"for when it gets colder."

"That reminds me," Nate put in. "The Dame does
the laundering tomorrow afternoon, so if you bring
your dirty things down to me, I'll see that she washes
them."

"Won't she notice them?"

He shook his head. "I shouldn't think so. With washing for twenty, what's an extra garment or two? She
doesn't sort them or anything. Once they're dry, she
just heaps everything up and we have to go through
and find our own stuff. Besides, most of what you're
wearing belongs to us, anyway."

"You're right." She laughed as she smothered a
yawn. "I'm going up, I guess."

"Do you want someone to light your way?" Geoffrey
asked.

She shook her head. "I can manage in the dark,
thanks. Goodnight."

"G'night," they echoed as she went out on silent
feet.

"Well, Geoffrey, are you going to make a try at Kenton's exercises?"

Geoffrey shrugged. "Naw. I'll just face the music, so
to speak. But you know, I've been thinking —"

"That's a first," Randall jibed.

"— about our Pup."

"Oh? And?"

"Well, she's —"

"Y'know," Orlando cut in "we should all get into the habit of calling Pup 'him.' Otherwise, someone's likely to overhear us, and we'll all be at sea without sails."

"You have a point," Randall agreed. "Go on, Geoffrey."

"I overheard something today on our way to Gram's. Two old geezers were talking in the street. Sir Henry Tuckfield's dead, shot by a *poacher*, and his daughter's disappeared — vanished, gone. Nate, what did Pup say her real name was? Do you remember?"

"Alice, wasn't it?"

Geoffrey nodded. "But was it Alice Tuckfield?"

"I don't know. I wasn't really paying attention. It might have been."

"Geoffrey, just what are you getting at?" Randall said brusquely.

"Do you remember the time Master Hollis gave us that lecture about discretion?"

The others nodded.

"And do you remember who he used for an example?"

Nate nodded. "Sir Henry Tuckfield. How did he describe him? 'A gifted musician without a grain of common sense who seems constitutionally incapable of holding his tongue.'"

"That's the one," said Geoffrey. "And Master Hollis went on to say Sir Henry would get himself in trouble with the Queen — musician or no — if he couldn't learn to be a little more circumspect. Now, I don't know if he mended his ways, but if Henry Tuckfield was shot by a poacher, would his daughter disappear? And if he *wasn't*, would his daughter be in danger?"

Randall frowned. "It's rather farfetched, don't you think, Geoff? Besides, if Tuckfield's daughter is in danger, it's probably better if none of us knows anything about it. He was a bad lot, I think — a Papist, according to rumor — and that's treason."

"But no one could be foolish enough to accuse an eleven-year-old girl of treason!" Geoffrey protested.

"Then she's probably not in any danger," Randall said patiently.

"Well, at least not from the Queen," Orlando put in eagerly, his eyes bright. "But what if the Queen wasn't behind it? What if it was a group of wicked courtiers, and —"

"Don't encourage him, Orlando!" Randall said. "It all sounds like a romance. I never told you this: my name is really Plantagenet and I'm the rightful heir to the throne. Be reasonable!"

Geoffrey's chin came up and he glared at Randall. "But —"

Randall held up one hand and spoke almost sharply. "Listen to me! Even if there *is* a plot — and it all sounds ridiculous to me — it's much safer for all of us *and* Pup if we don't know anything about it."

There was a short, tense silence. Finally, Geoffrey sighed.

"I suppose you're right, Randall. But I can't help wondering."

CHAPTER FIVE

"This is one of the things we'll be doing Christmas Eve," Master Frost announced in rehearsal as some music was passed out. "Let's read through it."

Master Kenton gave pitches and they began. The piece was different from the other things they had been rehearsing, Alice decided. The lines arched and intertwined, producing sounds sweet and compelling. In the wonder of this new music Alice lost the last vestiges of her timidity; her voice soared in a silver arc of sound as the line ascended. She broke off abruptly. Her heart gave a tremendous lurch, for Master Frost had stopped, his hands motionless in the air while he stared at her intently.

"Who the devil are you?" he burst out at last.

She could only stare at him with frightened brown eyes while her jaw flapped helplessly.

He waited for a few moments, but it was clear Alice was too taken aback to answer, so he shrugged and said, only a little impatiently, "Well, never mind. I'll see you after the rehearsal. Now, from the top of the second page . . ."

The rest of the rehearsal was awful. Alice could not concentrate. And though Geoffrey gave her an encouraging grin and Orlando patted her knee reassuringly, she could not help feeling that shortly she would again be out in the streets. As the rehearsal came to an end and the boys started out, Geoffrey leaned over and whispered, "I'll wait outside for you. Chin up, Pup. He won't bite."

She smiled weakly at him and watched him go. He was one of the last to leave. When Master Kenton rose to follow the others out, Master Frost shook his head slightly.

"Stay, won't you please, Hugh."

Without a word, the accompanist sat back down at the keyboard. Master Frost gestured Alice to stand beside the instrument; he took a seat in the front row and looked at her inquiringly.

"Well, young fellow, what is your name?"

"Pup, sir," she replied.

"Very well, Pup. Sing for me."

"S-sing?" She gasped. "What should I sing?"

"Whatever you like," he replied.

Alice's mind went blank; she couldn't even think of a folk song. Helplessly, she watched Master Frost's expression begin to change from expectancy to impatience. In desperation, she opened her mouth and began to sing anything at all just to break the silence.

At first the notes tumbled over each other a little, then steadied. She knew this: it was the piece they'd been rehearsing earlier, the one for Christmas Eve. She almost fancied she could hear the other parts. She *could* hear the other parts; Master Kenton had picked up the threads on the virginal and was accompanying her. When they finished, Master Frost nodded curtly, but Master Kenton stared at her through slightly narrowed eyes. Alice shifted uncomfortably.

"Range," said Master Frost at last.

Master Kenton played one of the patterns they used in the warmup, then nodded to Alice. She began to sing and together they ascended. Abruptly, Master Frost stopped them.

"That's high enough. Hugh, find him something to read."

Master Kenton shoved a piece of music at Alice. She looked at it in dismay. The treble part was intricate and the tempo fast. Master Kenton began to play, then stopped when Alice failed to come in.

"Whenever you're ready," he said with faint mockery, "I'll start again."

Alice flushed. This time she came in at the right time but floundered a bit over the pitch. Then she steadied herself mentally, and things went smoothly for a moment or two before she again ran into trouble. Master Frost cut her off with a wave of his hand.

"Enough of that. Something easier, please, Hugh."

Her heart sank. Master Kenton shoved another piece

of music at her, gave her a pitch and a nod, and began to play; she joined in. That *was* easier, she thought with relief as they finished, and she looked a little hopefully at Master Frost for some sign of approval, but his face was set in a faint frown.

"Now," Master Frost said, "Master Kenton will play a phrase, then you are to sing it."

Master Kenton began. At first the phrases were simple, but they rapidly became more involved and longer. Finally Master Frost signaled enough. She looked from one to the other anxiously; she thought that last one had been correct, but she couldn't tell from their faces.

"Do you play?" Master Frost asked.

"Play?" she repeated, at a loss.

"Virginal," he prompted impatiently.

"No, sir." Her heart sank further.

"Have you ever sung in a church choir before this?"

"No, sir," she said, feeling very inexperienced.

"What were you doing in my rehearsal, anyway?"

"We . . . *I* thought it would be a lark to see how long I could be in the choir before you noticed me," she replied steadily.

Master Kenton was startled into a bark of laughter; Master Frost frowned at him.

"You thought you could pass unnoticed in my choir?" Master Frost said. He and Master Kenton exchanged looks and shook their heads. Suddenly, Alice remembered one of the boys saying, "He'll never notice you so long as you don't sing flat," and she wondered if they would beat her before they turned her out into the street.

Master Frost motioned to Alice. "Come over here. I want a good look at you."

Alice's stomach rolled over slowly, but she approached without hesitation. The master studied her face; she wondered if he could hear her heart thumping. Can he tell I'm not a boy? she thought.

"How old are you?"

"Eleven, sir."

He frowned. "Are you from York?"

"No, sir. I grew up in London."

"Who taught you to sing?"

"Master William Hunnis."

His eyebrows shot up, and he exchanged a significant look with Master Kenton. Then he rose and went to the desk in one corner of the room. He took a quill from its stand, mended it, and dipped it in the inkwell.

"I must write a note to the Dean, explaining the situation."

"The D-Dean?" Alice repeated, her eyes wide with alarm.

"Of course the Dean," he replied a little testily. "I can hardly deal with you without his sanction. What's your real name?"

Alice swallowed hard. "Al-Alister Tucker."

He nodded and went back to his task. The quill scraped on the paper. Alice raised frightened dark eyes to Master Kenton's face. For a moment their eyes met, then the master smiled a little crookedly.

"Oh, for the love of heaven, Adrian, put the poor lad out of his misery. He thinks you're asking Father Boyce to excommunicate him or something."

Master Frost looked at Alice in amazement. "Excommunicate you? With your voice — and in time for Christmas? You ridiculous boy, of course not! I'm writing to arrange for your housing. The Dean will have to see that that harpy — Dame Anne? Agatha? Whatever her name is — is paid for your room and board."

She stared uncomprehendingly at him for a few moments. Then she began to feel weak with relief, but the master's next words brought her up short.

"Hugh, go fetch that rascal, Geoffrey."

She looked up with all the innocence she could muster. "What has he to do with this?"

Master Kenton fixed her with a long, sarcastic look. "You really don't have a very high opinion of our intelligence, do you?" he said acidly. Then he went out.

A few moments later, he returned with Geoffrey in tow. The boy winked at Alice, ignoring the masters' stern expressions.

"Well, Geoffrey Fisher," Master Frost began ominously, "what have you to say for yourself?"

"It was a grand prank," he replied unrepentantly, "though I must say, sir, I never thought you'd catch on so quickly."

"You were ill advised. I may forget names and faces,

but I do rather better with voices. But what I'd like to know is why you didn't tell Pup here to come around and audition for me, instead of fooling about with this rigmarole."

Geoffrey shrugged, then smiled impishly. "That would have been too tame, sir."

"Tame?" Master Frost boomed. "I'll give you tame! Now listen here, you impudent little rascal, this is a serious business. We make music in a cathedral, not a tavern or a theater. You have no business playing pranks for your own amusement, pranks that endanger the smooth operation of our —"

"Authority," Hugh Kenton put in wryly.

"Yes! Well — no." Master Frost suddenly began to laugh. "You're an awful scamp, Geoffrey," he said in a much milder tone. "And in punishment for your irreverence, you shall take charge of Pup and look out for him. Where are you staying, Pup?"

"With friends," she responded promptly.

"Can they put you up for a day or two more? There won't be a problem with Father Boyce, but it may take a little time."

She nodded.

"Good, then. Run along now, or you won't get lunch before your lessons. Oh, and Pup?" he called as the two opened the door.

"Sir?"

"How long *were* you in the choir before I noticed you?"

Alice grinned. "Nearly a week, sir."

Master Frost smiled ruefully and shook his head. Master Kenton laughed out loud. As the door shut, both men exchanged glances. "I don't believe it," Master Frost said, shaking his head. "Such a voice, by God."

"And such an ear," Master Kenton added. "You know, I think I'll write to Hunnis. I'd like to know more about this remarkable student of his."

"Yes, do. I'm curious as well."

"Why, in heaven's name, didn't he take the boy for the Chapel Royal?" Master Kenton wondered aloud, but Master Frost was no longer listening.

"We ought to do that lovely setting of 'On Christmas Night,' the one with the treble solo, and perhaps you could come up with something, too. His voice would blend beautifully with Emery's tenor, or . . ." He trailed off and looked at Kenton questioningly.

Kenton nodded. "Yes, of course, Adrian," he said brusquely as he rose. "I'm off to lunch now. Will you come?"

"Thank you, no," Frost replied, rising from his desk and taking the note. "I must see the Dean, if he's available."

Once outside in the streets, Geoffrey let out a terrific whoop and seized Alice's hands. They swung about in a wild dance for a moment or two, then stopped, laughing and panting.

"You're one of us!" Geoffrey exulted. "Official sanction and all. You'll even be able to eat with us!"

Alice frowned worriedly. "But, but won't the Dame

59

think it odd? I mean, won't I have to sleep in the second-floor room with all you boys?"

"Well, yes," Geoffrey admitted. "But you know, you can have one of the washing alcoves for yourself. You can change in there."

She looked a little skeptical, but her doubts could not withstand Geoffrey's enthusiasm and high spirits.

"I shall introduce you to the Dame — she might even give you lunch if she's in a good mood — and tell the others about the 'new boy.' Did you give old Frost a real name?"

"Yes. Alister. It was all I could think of," she added apologetically.

He laughed. "Even the Dame will call you Pup, I predict. Alister, forsooth. Alister what?"

"Tucker."

A few minutes later Geoffrey opened the kitchen door and they both strode boldly in. Alice was quick to note that Dame Agnes was out of the room, but the younger boys looked up curiously.

"Heavens, Geoffrey," Randall remonstrated, "are you out of your mind?"

"It's all right, Randall. This is Alister Tucker, but he likes to be called Pup. He's new. An official member," he added with a triumphant grin. Morris looked up, shock and outrage on his face, but Geoffrey went on, unheeding. "After having sailed through a rigorous audition with ease —"

"Ease?" Alice interrupted indignantly. "I thought they were going to beat me. It was awful."

Randall smiled a little reminiscently. "I remember mine. They asked me all sorts of questions I couldn't begin to answer and afterward asked to see my father. I thought they were going to upbraid him for wasting their time with an imbecile."

Alice nodded. "And then Master Frost said he was going to write a note to the Dean. I was terrified."

"Oh, poor Pup," Orlando said. "He should have known better. And I'll bet Sourface Kenton just sat there and sniggered in his sleeve, too."

"Well, actually, no," she said. "He told Master Frost to put me out of my misery, that I thought he wanted the Dean to excommunicate me or something."

There were low whistles.

"That's not like Sourface at all," Timothy said. "He must have been impressed with you."

"Maybe, maybe not," Geoffrey said. "But how about lunch? Is there anything left? And will one of you get the Dame? She should meet the new boy."

Soon the introduction was over. Dame Agnes had smiled at her new charge, said she'd be glad to have him — by which she meant, Nate explained later, she'd be glad to have the fee for his room and board — and said he could have lunch today, but not to count on another meal with them until the formalities had been completed. Then she smiled again at Alice and took herself off.

"Well," Orlando whispered, "that's another shoal avoided. It ought to be clear sailing from now on."

Alice looked up from her stew. "I certainly hope

you're right. But would someone please tell me about the masters at the school and what I'll be expected to do."

"Today," said Randall, since Geoffrey was too busy eating to reply, "I think they'll all just want to give you a poke and a prod to see what you know and find your levels. It will probably take them the rest of the week to assign you to classes and work out your schedule. But anyway, there's Master Hollis to teach us History and Geography, Music Theory with either Emery Morcocke — you met him on Sunday — or Master Kenton, depending on your level, Philosophy and Classics with Master Bennett —"

Alice choked. "Oh no! Latin, you mean?"

He nodded. "And Greek."

"I'm in trouble," she moaned. "I don't know any."

Timothy spoke up reassuringly. "They'll just put you with the beginning level. I hadn't had any Latin when I came, either."

Alice smiled at him gratefully. "What else?"

"Church History with Father Cooper," Randall continued. There were groans from some of the others. "Singing with Master Barnstable, Keyboard and Music History with Master Benbowe, Natural History with Master Williams, Sums with Master Mallin and Reading with Master Neste. That's all."

"All?" Alice repeated, appalled. "With so many lessons, I'm surprised we have time to sing! Whose idea was it to school the choirboys, anyway?"

Geoffrey pulled the corners of his mouth down,

tucked his chin in, and looked down his nose. "The cathedral choir," he began in his best Father Cooper voice, "was established over four hundred years ago, but the choir school is a recent innovation. Thanks to the generosity of our patroness, Lady Andrewes, our choirboys are not only taught to sing but are given a basic education that will assist them in whatever career they decide to pursue in later life. But come on," he added, dropping the pose. "We'd better be going."

CHAPTER SIX

When they reached the choir school, they went up a flight of stairs and down a corridor to a door that was slightly ajar. When Geoffrey tapped on it, the murmuring stopped and a deep voice called out, "Come in."

Geoffrey pushed the door open and went in with Alice. "Hello, Master Hollis," he said to a tall man standing just inside. "This is Pup. He's new. Master Frost said I was to bring him to you."

"Pup?" Master Hollis repeated.

"Well, Alister, really," she told him. "Alister Tucker, but Pup for short."

The master nodded. "Welcome. I'm Master Hollis. I teach History. And this is Master Bennett, Master Williams and Master Neste. How old are you?"

"Eleven, sir."

He nodded, then turned to the others. "I'll take him first. When I'm done, I'll send him to you, Edgar."

Master Bennett nodded.

Master Hollis turned back to Alice. "You come along with me. I'll give you some questions to answer so I can place your level. Thank you, Geoffrey. You may go."

Geoffrey winked at Alice before he went back downstairs. Alice followed in Master Hollis's wake to a classroom. Master Hollis sat down at a large desk, wrote several questions on a piece of paper, then gave the sheet to her.

"Take a seat in the back," he told her. "There's paper and ink at the desks. Here's a quill. Do your best with these questions. Some of them are rather difficult."

"Yes, sir," she said, then went to the back to work. The questions weren't too bad, she decided. Her father had seen to it that she was taught a fair amount of history so he would have someone to argue with, and one of her governesses had thought geography was a necessity. Alice could still remember painstakingly making maps. While she was working, some boys came in and Master Hollis began to lecture, but she paid no attention. After perhaps half an hour, she went to the front of the classroom and laid her paper on the desk. Master Hollis broke off and smiled at her.

"Thank you, Pup. Now, go to Master Bennett. He's right across the hall."

Master Bennett was a lean, dry little man with very dark eyes and a long nose that made him look a little like a field mouse. His room was utterly still except for the scratch of quill on paper as the boys there did exercises.

"Ah, yes," he said as Alice came in. "The new boy. Here you are." He handed her a sheet with some sentences written out in elegant script.

Alice took the sheet and went to a seat. She gazed at the words in dismay. Some of the Latin looked familiar from texts she had sung, but most of it made no sense. She translated the few words she recognized and made guesses at some of the others, but that didn't take very long. While she sat, wondering what to do, she became aware of Master Bennett's eyes on her.

"Finished already?" he asked. "Let me see."

Reluctantly, she took the paper up to him. He looked it over, then looked up at her. "Well, I won't have any trouble placing your level. Haven't you had any Latin? I should have thought a boy your age would have had *some*."

"No one has ever been able to make it sink in," she told him in a timid voice.

"I see," he said. "I trust I will have more success. But now, go on to Master Neste. He's in the third room on the left."

And so it went. Alice was passed from master to master for the rest of the afternoon; some of the subjects were easy for her (she had always loved to read; and though she hadn't loved numbers, she had been thoroughly drilled) while others were more difficult. But she didn't begin to feel comfortable until she saw the music masters.

She was sent first to Master Barnstable, the singing master. He was an excitable man, rather stout, with large hands that he waved expressively. At first Alice was a little afraid of him. He seemed rather offended that he had not been at her audition, but when she sang for him, his manner changed.

"I absolve him," he said with a sweep of his hand. "I utterly absolve him. Such a voice. Such a voice, by God! Where on earth did you spring from? You haven't been in York all these years?"

"No. I'm from London."

"London! Then why, for the love of heaven, aren't you in the Chapel Royal?"

"I . . ." Alice thought frantically. "My father was an old friend of Master Hunnis's, and he especially asked that I not be allowed in. Father thought music, even church music, rather frivolous."

Master Barnstable shook his head. "And Hunnis agreed to it?"

"On the condition that Father let him teach me to sing." It sounded rather lame to her — and she knew that both her father and Master Hunnis would have been horrified — but Master Barnstable let the story stand.

"I can't believe it," he murmured, sounding a little dazed. "Such a voice!"

"You like it, sir?" Alice asked a little doubtfully.

"Like it? Like it?" he demanded, flinging his arms wide. "You idiotic boy! It is, it is . . . There are no adequate words. It is . . . beautiful. But," he barked, pointing at her so abruptly that she jumped, "there is room for improvement! I shall see you twice a week."

"Twice a week, sir?"

"Yes. And now you must see Master Benbowe. The second door on the right."

Master Benbowe was nearly the opposite of Master Barnstable. He was a placid young man with a cheerful face and a friendly smile.

"So you're Pup," he said. "When Emery told me about you, I wondered why I hadn't seen you. Is it true you were in the choir a week before Master Frost noticed you?"

She nodded.

"Quite a good prank. Now, have you had any keyboard instruction?"

"Not to speak of. I know what the notes are, but that's about all."

He motioned her to the bench of the virginal. "Play a major scale on D, please."

Alice picked out the correct notes with one finger. Master Benbowe smiled. "Thank you. Now, what about music history? Have you been taught any?"

She nodded.

He rattled several questions at her in quick succession, all of which she answered with ease. "Very good," he said. "You're easy to place."

"I don't have to write anything down for you?"

He shook his head. "You'll be in the beginning level of keyboard and the advanced level of music history. But now I'm afraid you have to go see Master Kenton." His smile went a little wry. "We save the best for last. He's next door. Good luck."

"Thank you, sir."

Geoffrey, Nate, Randall and Orlando were struggling over some exercises in Master Kenton's room when she arrived. They looked up at her sympathetically as Master Kenton handed her two sheets of music paper.

"Do the first set of exercises," he told her curtly, "and correct the second. If it's too hard for you, don't waste my time. Tell me and I'll send you to Emery."

She sat down and went to work. The exercises were not very hard, and soon she was done. She raised her hand.

"Too hard?" Master Kenton asked, coming toward her.

"No, sir. I'm finished."

He took the sheets and looked through them. His eyebrows rose. "Too easy," he said at last. He went back to the desk and returned a moment later with another sheet. "Realize the figured bass," he ordered, then turned away.

Alice did. She had always liked doing realizations, though more than once Master Hunnis had chided her for, as he put it, letting her ear run wild. She knew, as she worked, that she ought to keep the realization austere and completely correct, but there were a few places where she just couldn't bring herself to be so unimaginative. There were several intricate little flourishes in her exercise by the time she finished with it. She looked up to find Master Kenton watching her. He held out his hand for the sheet and she gave it to him. As he studied it, his closed, somewhat sour expression changed grad-

69

ually to one of incredulity. He got up and stalked over to the virginal. As he played through the exercise, Alice listened critically.

"Come here," he said sharply.

She got up and went over to him. She stood quietly while he studied her searchingly.

"Have you had much composition?" he asked finally.

"A little, sir."

"Can you write a galliard?"

"I've never tried, sir, but I think I could."

"Do you think you could write an a capella anthem for six voices?" His tone was sarcastic.

"I could try," she said, "but I'd rather start with something less complex."

He studied her for a moment, then shook his head. "You'll be bored in the advanced group until we start composition in the spring, but the extra practice won't hurt you any. Have you seen Master Benbowe?"

"Yes, sir."

"Then you'd better stay here until the Evensong rehearsal. See if you can help Orlando."

She looked over at Orlando, who nodded enthusiastically. She pulled a chair up to his desk and settled down to offer aid.

"Where did you learn so much theory, Pup?" Orlando whispered.

"My singing master made me learn it," she replied.

"I hope he was more patient than old Sourface." Orlando's mutter was barely audible even to her.

"Pup!" Master Kenton barked suddenly.

They both jumped guiltily.

"Why the devil didn't Hunnis teach you to play the virginal?" he demanded.

Alice shrugged a little sadly. "My father wouldn't permit it. I never understood why, really. I suppose he thought it was inappropriate for a" — she caught herself barely in time — "for any son of his." Then, belatedly remembering what she had told Master Barnstable, she added, "He thought music rather frivolous and he wouldn't permit any argument. All he would say was, 'I forbid it and you will obey me in this.' "

"Narrow-minded fool," Kenton growled.

Any more questioning was forestalled by the cathedral bell tolling four. They all swept their papers into their satchels and made their escape, leaving Master Kenton still scowling.

"Well, did you brush through all right?" Nate asked as soon as they were out of the room.

"I think so. Bennett, Williams and Father Cooper probably think I'm awfully slow, but I think I did fairly well with everyone else."

"What did Master Barnstable say?" Randall asked.

She smiled. "A great deal — and in a loud voice."

"He liked you, then," Geoffrey reassured her. "He only talks softly to people who bore him. I was afraid he'd be offended that old Frost had signed you on without so much as asking his opinion."

"I think he must have been, for after I sang for him, he said, 'I absolve him. I utterly absolve him.' "

The others laughed at her mimicry.

"We'd better go," Geoffrey said suddenly. "Old Frost may want to talk to you before the rehearsal. Come on."

After the service, the boys began to leave in a chattering mob except for Morris, who hung about while Master Frost and Master Kenton spoke together. When Timothy happened to return, looking for his hat, he noticed Morris.

"Walk with me, Morris," he suggested cheerfully.

"I . . ." Morris looked at the two masters, still deep in conversation, then at Timothy. "Oh, all right," he said brusquely and the two boys left together. The others were out of sight.

"Morris, you were going to tell about Pup, weren't you?" Timothy asked him quietly.

Morris looked at him. "I was, Tim," he said at last. "Pup doesn't belong here. It's wrong."

"She doesn't have anywhere else to go."

"That doesn't make it right. Tim, she's a *girl!* She doesn't belong in the choir, and she shouldn't be living with all us boys."

Timothy looked at the older boy helplessly. "Morris, Pup isn't doing any harm, and she has a good voice. I know you don't approve, but Geoffrey and the others agreed to leave you out of it. Can't you just hold your tongue?"

Morris shook his head vehemently.

"Why are you being so spiteful?" Timothy asked. "Are you jealous of Pup?"

"No!" Morris cried, but his voice cracked on the

word. Morris clapped one hand over his mouth, his expression stricken.

"Oh, Morris!" Timothy cried in quick concern. "When did you start breaking?"

"Oh, shut up," he retorted. "I don't need your sympathy."

Timothy wisely closed his mouth and they walked the rest of the way in silence.

That night, Alice lay awake for a long time; it was her last night in the cupboard on the third floor. Master Frost had told her that, first thing in the morning, a letter from the Dean would be delivered to Dame Agnes arranging for her room and board. Earlier that evening, Geoffrey had taken her on a brief tour of the boys' quarters. He had shown her the bare upstairs schoolroom, where many of the boys did their lessons, and the rooms where they slept. There were three rooms, each with seven beds. Fortunately for Alice, the older boys shared a room and there was room for her in it. Geoffrey had shown her the bed they had selected for her, a cot tucked into a nook beneath a window, partially screened from the rest of the room and next to one of the washing alcoves; there were two in each bedroom, so the boys had agreed she could have this one to herself. There was a chest at the foot of the bed for her clothes and a small shelf by the head for her books. It would be more comfortable than the cupboard, Geoffrey had assured her, but Alice knew she would miss the privacy of her little nest in the garret. She rolled over and sighed. At least she was an official member of the choir even if she did have to learn Latin. She started to review the masters in her mind, but before she got very far into the list she was asleep.

The next morning after Matins, Timothy sought out Master Frost. The choirmaster took one look at his worried face and motioned him to a seat. "What's on your mind, Timothy?"

Timothy took a deep breath. "It's Morris. I'm worried about him. He's been acting very strangely lately. For one thing, he's very jealous of Pup. I know Morris isn't the friendliest person, but sir, that's really not like him. I think there's something else bothering him."

Master Frost raised his eyebrows. "Any idea what?"

"He hasn't spoken to you?"

"No."

Timothy sighed. "He'll probably be angry with me for telling you this, but Master, I think his voice is breaking."

The master ran a hand through his hair and sighed. "I'll speak to him, Timothy. I hope I can reassure him that he won't just be cast aside. Thank you for telling me."

"You're welcome, Master." Timothy rose and left, concealing a sigh of relief. Now, if Morris said something, perhaps Master Frost wouldn't believe him.

Three days later, Morris was gone. He had been apprenticed as a clerk to a merchant. Before he left, he found Timothy to say farewell. Timothy was relieved to find him smiling.

"Well, I'm going, Tim," Morris told him.

"You're not too unhappy, are you, Morris?" Timothy asked.

Morris shook his head. "Master said I could come sing for him once my voice had finished changing, so I may be back one day."

"Did you tell him about Pup?"

Morris laughed. "No. He wouldn't let me. Every time I mentioned Pup, he'd interrupt." He looked at Timothy shrewdly. "Did you have something to do with that?"

"Me?" Timothy said, dripping innocence, then he laughed. "God keep you, Morris."

"And you, Timothy."

It wasn't long before Alice began to feel as though she'd been at the choir school all her life. There was something comforting in the predictability of each day — service, rehearsal, lessons, service — and it was wonderful to be surrounded by music and musicians. She even found that learning Latin was not half the chore she had feared it would be.

After Evensong one night, as the choristers were all going home to supper, Alice stopped short, slapping her forehead. "Bother! I left my Church History essay in the choir room. I'd better go back and get it. Don't wait for me." She turned away and ran lightly back down the lane.

When she arrived outside the room she was surprised to hear music. It was Master Kenton. She could see him in the inadequate light of the single candle burning on the music rack. She slipped through the open door, intending to retrieve her things and tiptoe away, but once inside she stood in the shadows, listening with wonder to the intricate, powerful music that poured from the virginal. She had never heard anything like it. How long she stood there, enmeshed in the music, she didn't know, but it was over all too suddenly. Almost before she realized that he had stopped playing, Master Kenton was standing in front of her, glaring down at her.

"What the devil are you doing here?" he demanded furiously.

It took her a moment to recover herself. "I'm sorry, sir. I didn't mean to startle you. I came in here to get some things I left behind. When I heard you playing, I stopped to listen."

"A likely story." Though his face was in shadow and she couldn't see his expression, she could hear the sneer in his voice. "I'd like to know why you were sneaking about."

"I wasn't sneaking about," she protested. "When I came in here to get my essay, I didn't mean to stay. I wouldn't have stayed except, except . . ."

"Except what?" he prodded. "And make it good."

"Except for your playing — not just what you were playing, but the way you played it. I've never heard anything like it, anything so . . . so alive, so beautiful —

like you'd translated emotion to sound without any hitches, or — oh, I can't put it into words."

"Someone," he said, his tone cynical, "ought to have warned you that I'm immune to flattery."

"I wasn't flattering you," she insisted.

"No?" The contempt in his voice flicked her raw.

"No!" Her temper flared. "It's the truth — though how such a sour old man can make such incredible music is a mystery to me!" She started toward the door, but Master Kenton caught her arm.

"Sit down," he ordered curtly.

Alice sat, her hot flush of anger replaced by a sick feeling in her stomach. Now I've done it, she thought. Master Kenton lit some more candles, then came to stand in front of her, studying her minutely. At last he sighed.

"I owe you an apology, Pup."

"Y-you owe m-me . . ." she began. "But I should never have said what I did."

"Why not?" His smile was a little crooked. "I *am* a sour old man."

"But sir, it isn't for me to take you to task." Someday, she thought, my temper is going to get me into real trouble. She was surprised he wasn't angrier; perhaps he wasn't as sour as he acted.

For a long moment he stood looking down at her, his expression inscrutable; then he said a little gruffly, "I know I'm a fool to do this, but you seem to have a true appreciation of music. I'll teach you to play, Pup, if you like."

Alice gaped at him. "If I like," she repeated. "Oh, sir!"

"I take it that means yes. Very well, tomorrow I'll arrange it with Benbowe. You'll have to practice for me, you know."

"Oh, I will."

"You've missed your supper. If you like, you can come along with me."

"I'd better get back," she said with a little regret. "They will have saved something for me."

"I hope you're right. Have you got your essay?" he added as he turned to put out the candles.

"Yes, sir. Goodnight, sir."

"Goodnight, Pup."

She fairly flew back to the dormitory. The washing up was done except for a place set at the table. Geoffrey and Nate were arguing when she came in, but when they saw her they dropped the subject.

"What kept you?" Nate asked. "We were just trying to decide whether to go looking for you."

"Kenton," she replied. "He was in the choir room when I went in for my stuff."

"Practicing, you mean?" Geoffrey asked. "Good Lord, you didn't go in anyway, did you?"

She nodded.

"And lived to tell the tale!" Nate said. "Someone should have warned you, Kenton's a real bear when he's practicing — and he's bad enough most of the time! Did he see you? Was he angry?"

She nodded. "I thought he was going to murder me

at first, and then he made me angry by calling me a flatterer when I was sincere."

"Wait a minute," Geoffrey said. "Back up. Pup, did you stay and listen to him?"

"Yes! He's a fabulous musician. I . . . Geoffrey, I couldn't leave."

Geoffrey and Nate whistled.

"He wanted to know why I was there, so I told him, and I told him what I thought of his playing, and he called me a flatterer, and I lost my temper."

"What did you say?" Geoffrey asked, his eyes wide.

"I said, 'It's the truth — though how such a sour old man can make such incredible music is a mystery to me!' "

"Dear heaven," Nate whispered.

"But it turned out wonderfully," she concluded triumphantly. "Master Kenton is going to teach me to play "

"Kenton teach —" Geoffrey repeated numbly. "And you're happy? Pup, have you gone mad? Do you *want* old Sourface Kenton after you all the time? He'll never be satisfied with you. Never. You can't want that!"

"I want to be able to play like him," she said quietly. "If that's what it takes, then yes, I do want just that."

Both boys stared at her in amazement. "You know, Pup," Nate said at last, "either you're a true musician or a martyr. But eat your supper. I want to wash the plate."

CHAPTER SEVEN

Master Benbowe was closing up his virginal, preparing to leave for the day, when Emery poked his head in. "Hello, Charles," he greeted him cheerfully. "How were your monsters today?"

"Not so bad. Emery," he added questioningly, "how likely, in your opinion, would Kenton be to take on a keyboard student?"

"Not a chance in the world," he responded promptly. "Why, even when young Barshawe was here, Kenton wouldn't have anything to do with him, said he had better things to do than waste his time with some scrubby schoolboy — and Barshawe was good for his age, too."

Charles shook his head. "Then tell me what you make of this. Kenton walks into my beginning keyboard class and says in his inimitable way, 'Charles, I'd like a word with you. I'm going to relieve you of one of your students. Pup will study keyboard with me.' Then, without so much as a by-your-leave, he turned for the door and said, 'Come along, Pup.' And that was that. The boy went out on Kenton's heels, didn't even look back."

"Do you mean to say he took a student out of your *beginning* section?" Emery's voice rose with incredulity. "I don't believe it! I mean — Well, if you say so, but . . . but . . . ." He shook his head as though to clear it. "Kenton? I shouldn't think he'd be much of a teacher. God knows the man can play, but he has no patience. And his temper's rather frightening. I don't envy young Pup."

"Nor do I," Charles agreed with feeling.

"You know," Emery said, his sudden, roguish grin lighting his face, "I'd give quite a lot to observe one of the lessons!"

"Not I," Charles said. "I wouldn't have the stomach for it. I wonder what Adrian would make of this. If anyone could be said to know Kenton, it's he."

"We could go ask him," Emery suggested.

"Yes," Charles agreed with decision, "we could. Let's!"

They ran Master Frost to earth in the choir library, a small, cluttered room down the hall from the choir room. The master was standing on a stool, rooting about on some of the uppermost shelves, his back to the door.

"Hugh," he began without turning around, "have you any idea what happened to that set of Taverner anthems? I can't seem to find them." He turned then, dusting his hands on his tunic, and smiled a greeting at the two young men. "Oh, hello. You've heard about Hugh?"

"Well, yes," Charles replied a little sheepishly. "I can't help but wonder if he's gone a little mad. The new boy can't even play! What is Kenton thinking of?"

Master Frost smiled. "I couldn't believe it myself when he told me. But Hugh believes Pup has a sincere desire to learn."

"But even so," Emery protested, "I can't see Kenton in the role of a patient teacher. Surely young Pup has no idea what he's getting himself into."

"Oh, I think Pup has a very clear idea," the master replied dryly. "It's Hugh who deserves our . . . concern. Do you know, that little fellow called him a sour old man — to his face!"

Emery and Charles exchanged looks, then burst out laughing. "You know," Emery said at last, "Pup may be good for Kenton."

Master Frost smiled enigmatically. "I am very nearly certain of it."

As Alice was hanging up her cassock and surplice that night, Master Frost came over to her.

"Can you stay for a few minutes, Pup?" he asked.

She looked up, startled. "Of course, sir."

"I've asked Emery and Christopher Shepard to stay as well," he went on. "I've found some trios I'd like to try. We might do one for a Sunday evening service or for Christmas Eve."

"Sunday evening?" Alice asked. "I thought — I didn't think there was a service then."

"Oh yes," he said with a smile. "But we don't have the choir, just a small group. It gives people a rest."

"Some people," Master Kenton put in dryly as he came up to them.

Alice looked at him. "There's no rest for the wicked."

Master Kenton glared down at her sardonically. "I daresay you'd know."

"Oh no, sir," she said innocently. "I'm not wicked, just impudent."

He shook a finger warningly at her but made no comment. Emery had come up in time to catch the exchange, and he and Master Frost exchanged glances. Christopher Shepard joined them a moment later. He was a thin, colorless man with pale gray eyes and a rather weary smile. He looked around at them.

"Here or the choir room?" he asked.

Alice was startled by the rich power of his deep voice. It was totally unexpected. She looked at him in surprise; he caught her expression and smiled.

"Here," Master Frost replied as he handed them some music. Master Kenton gave pitches and they began. The first piece started with the treble alone. Alice listened to her voice as the sound sailed into the cathedral; then the others joined her, Emery's effortless tenor and Christopher's rich bass. The sounds twined about each other, displacing the silence the way a candle flame pushes back the darkness. When they finished, Master Frost nodded.

"That will work," he said. "Now, Pup, in that first phrase, build to the word 'joyful': 'Sing, O heavens; and be *joyful*, O earth' — that's where the phrase is going. Then you can taper a little on 'earth.' Emery and Christopher, come in a little more strongly: 'and break forth into singing O mountains' — it's quite a triumphant statement, really. Shall we try it again?"

Alice found singing with a small group exhilarating. She could have gone on all night, but finally Master Frost stopped.

"I've kept you longer than I meant to," he apologized. " 'Sing, O heavens' is for Sunday evening. We'll rehearse it again on Saturday after the service. I'd like to use you three on Christmas Eve as well. I'll see what I can find." He began gathering his things together.

Alice collected her books and papers, then went to the organ bench, where Master Kenton was changing his shoes. He straightened and looked down at her.

"Sir," she began, "I forgot to ask you earlier: when would be the best time for me to practice?"

Master Kenton considered. "I generally use the choir room after Evensong. I suppose you could use my classroom . . . but you have your dinner then, don't you? I tell you what. Why don't you use the choir room in the early morning?" His tone went suddenly cynical. "If you bestir yourself, you can get in some time before Matins as well as an hour between the service and the rehearsal."

"Oh, come, Hugh," Emery put in suddenly. "That's no good. He won't get any breakfast."

"Sacrifice is good for the soul," Kenton said shortly.

"Well, Adrian won't thank you if Pup faints away in rehearsal," he muttered defensively.

"When I want your advice, Emery, I will ask for it," Kenton told him coldly. With a quick, impatient movement, he swept all his music together, picked it up, and stalked off.

Emery sighed and shook his head, then looked down at Alice. "I never will learn to hold my tongue with him. See you tomorrow, Pup."

"Right," she agreed cheerfully, and with a little bounce in her step, she turned toward home.

The morning practice time turned out to work beautifully. Alice found that two hours of solitude was exactly what she needed to satisfy the part of her that missed her privacy. There were other advantages, too, the main one being that she was up, washed, and dressed before the Dame was stirring. Even the matter of breakfast had been satisfactorily settled: Dame Agnes left bread and cheese out for her, and in return Alice filled the woodbox and built up the kitchen fire before she left.

One morning when she went out to the woodshed, shivering in the cold darkness before sunrise, she heard a strange, plaintive noise that seemed to be coming from the back of the shed. She set the lantern carefully on the floor and crept around behind the woodpile to investigate. At first she could see nothing, though the sound grew a little louder; then, abruptly, the sound changed from a plaintive, unidentifiable whimper to an unmistakable meow. A small black and white kitten came toward her out of the shadows. It was limping and its coat was spattered with mud. Alice held out her hands to the little animal and it came to her, watching her warily with enormous yellow-green eyes. She picked it up, appalled to feel how thin it was under its coat. She tucked the little beast into her jacket, picked up the lantern, and went back inside.

She put the kitten on the hearth and looked about for something to feed it. She found the leftover fish stew from supper, spooned some into a bowl, and set it down for the kitten. It attacked the food, growling over it as though it were afraid she might try to take it back. Alice left the animal to its breakfast and went back out to the woodshed. By the time she had finished filling the woodbox, the kitten had finished its feast and its bath. Alice took the bowl, washed it, and put it away. Then she picked up the kitten and examined it.

"You'd better come with me," she told him. "Dame Agnes would not approve of you."

He blinked at her sleepily, then seemed to smile as she ran a finger under his chin. He was quite a handsome kitten, she thought — or he would be if he weren't so thin. His markings were almost perfectly symmetrical. The black on his back reached past his eyes, so he looked as though he was wearing a mask, but the rest of his face and his chest were white, as were each of his paws. Only one thing marred his symmetry: a small patch of black, like an off-center goatee, under half his chin. The kitten yawned then, displaying sharp white teeth and a long pink tongue. Alice smiled and tucked him into her jacket; then she went off to the choir room.

While she practiced that morning, the kitten slept curled up in her lap. She was beginning to wonder what she would do with him when the door opened and Geoffrey came in.

"Hi, Pup," he greeted her. "A fine morning, isn't it?"

His air was so casual that immediately she was suspicious. "You're early," she said. "What are you up to?"

He sighed in a melancholy way. "It's terrible the way no one trusts me. I rise early on a fine morning and — Hey! What's that? You've got a kitten! Where'd you find him?"

"In the woodshed. You don't suppose the Dame will let us keep him, do you?" she asked without hope.

" 'What?' " Geoffrey cried, mimicking Dame Agnes's shrill voice. " 'Keep a nasty, flea-bitten cat? Have you lost your senses?' "

"Then what can we do with him?" Alice asked. "I couldn't bear to put him back out in the cold."

Geoffrey thought for a while. "Maybe we could keep him in the cathedral. There's usually a door open during the day, so he could come and go. As long as we leave food for him, he ought to stay around. A church cat for church mice. Have you named him yet?"

Alice shook her head.

"We could call him Boots," he suggested.

The kitten opened one eye and looked reproachfully

up at Geoffrey. Alice laughed. "You can tell he doesn't think much of that."

Geoffrey grinned. "Well, how about Sloth? It suits him."

"I think," said Alice, "we should call him Catechism."

He laughed. "That's good. But come on. We've got to get him hidden before Matins."

"Where shall we hide him?" Alice asked, taking the kitten in her arms as she rose.

"How about the triforium? No one goes up there."

They set off. A few minutes later they were in the narrow passage behind the open arches that looked down on the nave. They found a sheltered nook for the kitten and set him down. Geoffrey emptied his satchel and laid it down on the floor.

"He can use that for a bed — for now, anyway. You stay here, Catechism," he instructed the cat, "and we'll bring you something to eat later."

Alice stroked his fur. "Be good, Catty." Then she and Geoffrey sauntered off to join the others for the service.

After lunch, Geoffrey and Alice raced up to the triforium with the scraps they had saved, but Catechism was not on his makeshift bed.

"What should we do?" she asked. "There isn't time to look for him. Do you suppose anything has happened to him?"

"I doubt it. He's probaby just exploring. Here's what we'll do. We'll leave the food here for him, then come back before Evensong and see if he's eaten it. But we'd better run or we'll be late." They laid the scraps in a little pile beside the satchel, then rushed downstairs and across the street to the school building. They parted company at the door, Geoffrey off to Master Bennett's room and Alice to her lesson with Master Barnstable.

They finished the afternoon, as always, in Theory with Master Kenton. Halfway through the class, when they were supposed to be doing a realization, Geoffrey leaned over to Alice and whispered, "Well, what do you think? Shall we tell them?"

"Tell us what?" Randall demanded in a whisper.

"Yes," Orlando added. "I thought you came into Bennett's out of breath and up to something. What's the secret?"

"Quiet," said Master Kenton.

"Blast you, Geoffrey," Randall hissed. "You knew that would happen!"

Geoffrey preserved a saintly silence.

"Geoffrey's just trying to get you into trouble. We'll tell you after class," Alice said.

"I said quiet!"

For the rest of the class they managed to behave, but almost before the cathedral bell had finished tolling four they were out in the hall, running for the stairs.

"What is it? What's the secret?" Nate demanded breathlessly.

"We'll show you," Geoffrey replied.

With Alice and Geoffrey in the lead, soon they were

all in the triforium. Catechism had returned, accepted their offering, and settled down for his afternoon nap. He was asleep when they arrived, sprawled in a very undignified way, but he woke up right away and sat regally while the introductions were performed.

"We've got to make him a better bed," Nate said. "A pillow would be best. Do you suppose there's a spare one in the Dame's linen closet?"

"I'll bet anything she counts them," Randall said. "We'd better think of something else. I have a shirt that's too small. Catechism could have that."

"I just thought of the perfect thing!" Geoffrey put in. "We'll get Catty a spare cassock. That'll make a great bed. And after all, the choir mascot should have choir garb."

Just then, the sound of the organ reminded them of their duties. After bidding Catechism farewell, they hurried away.

"I hope Catechism likes music," Nate remarked, "because he surely will hear a lot of it."

CHAPTER EIGHT

"Relax!" Master Kenton shouted at Alice at her lesson several days later. He strode angrily across the room, then back, glaring at her fiercely. "You can't possibly play with your shoulders hunched up about your ears and your fingers stiff as blocks of wood!"

"Then don't bellow at me," she protested. "I can't possibly relax if I'm frightened."

Kenton stopped his restless pacing and studied her. "I suppose you have a point," he admitted. "I'll try not to shout at you, but you must relax, Pup. If you are stiff and tense, your playing will be stiff and tense. Here, let your arms hang, so. That's right. Now shake your hands, shake the tension out. Good. Begin again . . ."

Alice played through the piece, a simple dance, and when she had finished Master Kenton nodded.

"Were you satisfied with that, Pup?"

She shook her head.

"Why not?" There was a challenge in his eyes. "The notes were right and your tempo was steady."

"But it's a dance, sir, and it sounded like an exercise."

"Very true. Now, Pup, when you sing, you make phrases by building in volume and intensity to the places that are important and tapering in the places that are not as important. You can't do that on the virginal; you have no range of dynamics with this instrument. There is sound or silence. So you must make your phrases with pauses, little hesitations to emphasize the sound that follows. Here, let me demonstrate . . ."

Alice moved over on the bench to make room for him. When the next class came in, they were still sitting side by side, engrossed in making music.

That evening after supper, Geoffrey and Alice sneaked out to visit Catechism. He greeted them enthusiastically, though he showed only a polite interest in the dainties they had brought him. By the light of the candle stub she had saved from the trash, Alice could see that the kitten had lost his pitiful leanness of just a few days before: his coat was sleek and his white whiskers immaculate.

"He must be catching mice," Geoffrey said. "I think he just eats the things we bring to please us. Or perhaps the verger's feeding him. Nate said he saw him patting Catechism."

Catechism rolled over on his back and waved a languid paw in the air. When they laughed at him, he righted himself abruptly, taking an extremely dignified pose and looking a little offended.

"See what I brought you, Catty," Alice said, taking out a piece of string with a wad of cloth tied to the end. She started down the narrow corridor, trailing the string tantalizingly behind her. At first Catechism held himself aloof; then his curiosity got the better of him and he pounced. They all tussled together until the candle stub began to flicker dangerously.

"We'd better go," Alice said reluctantly, winding up the toy and slipping it back into her pocket. She picked up the candle stub and they made for the stairs. Geoffrey started down, followed closely by Alice; she held the stub up high so they could both see by its flickering light. Suddenly, a faint sound came to her ears and her hand closed warningly on Geoffrey's shoulder. She put the candle out and stood frozen in the silence. There it was again: footsteps. They were coming nearer.

"Well, where the devil is he? He did say tonight, didn't he?"

All the blood seemed to rush from Alice's heart and she gripped Geoffrey's shoulder hard to keep from falling. She knew that voice: Sir Roderick Donne.

"That's what he told me," another voice replied. Lord Crofton, Alice thought, but she wasn't certain. "Damn him, he should be here! I told him the matter was urgent. You don't suppose he's planning to betray us?"

Sir Roderick's voice was grim. "Even he wouldn't

dare. It's much more likely he hasn't any news and doesn't want to admit it to us. I don't understand it. People don't just disappear."

"No. But it has occurred to me . . . We may be looking in the wrong area. The brat may have gone to London."

"How?" Sir Roderick retorted scathingly. "It's a damned long walk. Besides, if that is the case, we're finished. London's full of waifs, and the Queen —"

He broke off as they heard a door scrape open.

"That must be he," the other murmured, then his tone changed. "No, devil take it! It's the organist! Darken the lantern and let's be gone. We mustn't be found here. I shall see our friend on the morrow and get an explanation from him . . ." Their voices faded as they moved away until at last there was silence.

"Let's go," Geoffrey breathed.

Alice was rooted with fright and couldn't move.

Geoffrey tugged at her impatiently. "Come on, Pup. Let's get out of here."

She managed to nod and followed him down the rest of the stairs, groping her way in the dark. But as they left the shelter of the stairway a beam of light caught them, and they both froze for an instant.

"Pup! Geoffrey!" It was Master Kenton's voice. "What the devil are you doing here at this hour?"

Before either of them could reply, a small black and white shape came pelting down the stairs into the lantern light. Catechism arched his back and spat at the startled master. Geoffrey scooped the cat up and held him protectively. Kenton stared for a moment, then burst out laughing.

"The verger mentioned a cat. I should have guessed you two were involved. There's no need to look at me like that," he added gruffly. "I won't say anything about your pet. I just hope he has the sense to stay out of the way during the services." Suddenly, he held the lantern up and peered closely at Alice. "What's the matter, Pup? You're trembling."

"I'm c-cold," she told him. "Don't you feel it?"

He looked at her searchingly but spoke brusquely. "Hadn't you better be getting home? Dame Agnes will be worried about you."

"It's not as late as all that," Geoffrey cried, "is it?"

"It's well after nine."

"Lord have mercy," he murmured fervently. "She'll skin us."

"We can't have that," Kenton said dryly. "I'll come along with you and see if I can't smooth down her feathers."

Geoffrey gaped at him. "Th-thank you, sir."

When they were out on the street, Kenton turned to Alice. "Who were those men?"

"I — I don't kn-know, sir. We — we heard them talking when we were coming down the stairs. Th-they didn't sound as though they'd like being overheard, so we hid until they went away." The words came out in a rush. "They were to meet someone who didn't come, and they were talking about people disappearing, but it didn't make any sense."

Kenton looked from Alice to Geoffrey and back again, then shrugged. "I wonder who they could be meeting in the cathedral."

Shortly, they arrived at the dormitory. No sooner were they inside the door than the Dame began railing at them, oblivious to Kenton's presence.

"You wicked, naughty boys! Where have you been? How dare you sneak off like that, then stay out half the night? You deserve a beating —"

Master Kenton interrupted her tirade with a surprisingly graceful bow. "I beg your pardon, ma'am. We didn't mean to keep them so long, but there was something we needed to have correctly before the Eucharist tomorrow. Master Frost and I rather lost track of the time."

Dame Agnes was taken aback. "Oh. Well, of course." Then she recovered herself. "But the next time you two little scamps have to go out for a late rehearsal, make sure I know of it. I was quite worried for you."

"Yes, ma'am. We're sorry, ma'am," they murmured, hanging their heads.

"Well, see that it doesn't happen again."

"You'd better go straight up to bed, boys," Kenton put in sternly, "if you're going to be of any use tomorrow."

"Yes, indeed," the Dame agreed as Alice and Geoffrey made for the door. "And now, Master Kenton," she went on in a suddenly honeyed tone, "it was so kind of you to bring them back. I do hope you'll join me for a cup of tea."

"Madam, I should be delighted," he responded promptly. Geoffrey and Alice exchanged glances and covered their mouths to keep back giggles until they were out of earshot.

"Poor Master Kenton," Alice gasped once they'd reached the sanctuary of the second floor. "Martyred for our sakes!"

"Who would believe it?" Geoffrey crowed. "I didn't think old Sourface knew how to be civil, much less gallant!"

Alice could hear Geoffrey still sniggering over it while she changed into her nightshirt in the washing alcove. He whispered a goodnight to her, then all was still. Alice climbed into bed, but lay awake long into the night.

The next morning was the first Sunday of Advent, and Master Frost had warned them that the Archbishop of York would be in attendance. They had prepared some particularly challenging music, and everyone knew it was important that the service go smoothly. When the choir gathered in the south transept before the service, Alice found herself next to Randall. Both of them kept sneaking covert glances at the Archbishop.

"Will he preach, Randall?" she asked.

"I doubt it," Randall whispered back. "He usually preaches Christmas Day and Easter, if he's here. I think it's the Dean's turn — or Father Cooper's."

Alice sighed. The Archbishop looked so imposing in his lavish vestments, crowned by his miter and carrying his heavy crozier. An enormous amethyst ring glittered on one hand. Authority seemed to emanate from him; she was sorry she wouldn't hear him preach. Suddenly, she realized the Archbishop had noticed her interest and was looking back at her. She blushed, but the Archbishop smiled at her.

Master Kenton finished the prelude and the choir sang the introit. As they lined up for the procession, she noticed that Geoffrey maneuvered to be behind her in line. She looked over her shoulder to grin at him, but saw at once that something was wrong. Before she could ask any questions, the procession had begun. She had to hurry undignifiedly to catch up with Randall. When the choir was in place, she turned to Geoffrey.

"What's the matter?" she whispered as they finished the last verse of the hymn.

"It's Cathechism," he hissed back but got no further, for Master Frost had raised his hands to begin the Kyrie. Now there would be no chance to find out more until the Collects.

But as she knelt down after the Gloria, she saw what Geoffrey was worried about. There was a long black tail sticking out from beneath the hangings on the altar. She exchanged a horrified look with Geoffrey. There was nothing they could do. They couldn't even warn Nate, Randall and Orlando, for Randall and Orlando were on the other side of the choir and Nate was serving as an acolyte. Alice sent up silent prayers that no one would notice, that Catechism would stay out of sight for the rest of the service.

For a while everything went smoothly, though

neither Alice nor Geoffrey heard a word of the Dean's sermon. When he finished, they sang the Offertory anthem. While the Archbishop was consecrating the bread and wine, Alice saw the tail twitch. She held her breath all the way through the Lord's Prayer and sang the Agnus Dei barely able to watch Master Frost. The choir rose and went up to receive communion. The Archbishop gave the chalices to the Dean and Father Cooper and took up the paten. Then it happened. As the Archbishop started toward the waiting choristers with the Dean and Father Cooper following, Catechism emerged from beneath the altar hangings, looked at the Archbishop curiously, then cut behind him toward the nearest choirboys. Father Cooper, pacing solemnly in the Archbishop's wake, trod squarely on the kitten. Catechism yowled. Father Cooper jumped and cursed, nearly spilling the wine. With all his fur on end, the cat made a direct, frantic line for Alice, practically flinging himself into her arms, loudly voicing his grievances. The choirboys dissolved into muffled giggles. Alice clamped Catechism's jaws shut with one hand and tried to soothe him with the other. Father Cooper recovered his dignity and continued, but Alice saw his face. When it came her turn, she wondered if he would cram the silver chalice down her throat; but he contented himself with a smoldering glare at her and a rather sarcastic inflection to the ritual words. As she went back to her place, she hid Catechism under her surplice. She and Geoffrey exchanged looks as they sat back down, then found themselves stifling giggles.

The rest of the service passed without mishap. As soon as Alice and Geoffrey could, they ran lightly up to the organ loft to put their robes away.

"If we're quick," Geoffrey whispered, "we can get Catechism away before Father Cooper catches up with us."

"Can't we hide in the closet until he goes away?" Alice suggested.

"He'd find us," Geoffrey said regretfully. "Hurry up."

As they slipped downstairs they ran into Randall, who was just coming up. "You'll never make it. Father Cooper's at the door. Give me Catechism. I'll go out the other way while you distract him. I don't think he'll bother about the cat. It's *you* he wants, Pup."

Alice put the cat in his arms. "Pray for me," she murmured ruefully and went on down. Father Cooper was standing near the foot of the stairs, his arms crossed on his chest and a look of pure menace in his eyes. Alice swallowed hard, but stood her ground while the people left the cathedral. When almost everyone was gone, Father Cooper approached her with ominous dignity.

"What," he began, "was the meaning of that appalling incident? Don't you know better than to interrupt a service in the house of God?"

Alice raised her head defiantly. "It was an accident, Father. I'm terribly sorry it happened, but I don't really see how I could have prevented it."

"Oh, you don't?" he retorted sarcastically. "And how did that, that creature find its way into the cathedral?"

"I found him and brought him here because he was starving and Dame Agnes doesn't allow us to keep animals, but I never thought he'd cause a disturbance during a service. I thought he might even catch mice or do something useful."

"This cathedral," Father Cooper said primly, "is not a home for stray animals. Surely the impropriety, the enormous *irreverence*, of using a house of God so *must* have occurred to you. Surely, *surely* you must have felt a twinge in that lamentably underdeveloped part of your character called a conscience at the thought of thus *defiling* this cathedral."

Alice's temper flared. "As a matter of fact, Father, I did not. *My* conscience was appalled — as any true Christian's would be — at the thought of leaving one of God's creatures to starve in the streets! I don't believe for a moment that God minds having one small cat in His house, and if God doesn't mind, then who are you to complain, you *hypocrite?*"

There was a stunned silence. Then Father Cooper, quite red in the face, cried, "I shall report you to the Dean for your insolence!"

"Well, I don't care if you do! You *are* a hypocrite — and a *fat* one!"

The priest reached out suddenly and caught her wrist roughly. "I shall beat you myself, you impudent whelp!"

"That you won't, Father Cooper," said Master Frost firmly. He had been seated in the first row of choir stalls; now he approached the priest with deliberate footsteps. "The disciplining of the choirboys is my concern. You will, of course, report him to the Dean if you feel it necessary, but you shall *not* beat him. Release his arm."

Father Cooper did so, then, with one last venomous look at Alice, turned on his heel and stomped purposefully away.

"Now, Pup," Master Frost went on less sternly, "I understand your unwillingness to let that poor creature starve, but the cathedral *isn't* the place for a mischievous kitten. Some other arrangement must be made. Perhaps the verger will take it in — or one of the other choir members. Where is the animal now?"

"I'm not exactly sure," Alice admitted, reluctant to bring Randall or the others into it if she could avoid it.

"I've got it," said Master Kenton unexpectedly. He had come down after the postlude and had been leaning, unnoticed, against the choir screen. He was holding the kitten awkwardly. "And I'll take it in," he added gruffly.

Master Frost shot him a startled look, then smiled. "That will answer nicely, Hugh. Now, we should all go along to our dinners." His glance included Geoffrey, Randall, Nate and Orlando, who were loitering nearby. "You'll probably have to see the Dean later this afternoon," he added to Alice with a faint, reassuring smile. "He's a fair man, Pup, and not above being amused."

Alice swallowed hard and nodded, then went over to Master Kenton, who was waiting for her.

"Thank you, sir," she said.

"For what?" The master's tone was brusque. "I need a mouser, this creature needs a home. What do you call him, anyway?"

"Catechism."

He gave a bark of laughter. "*Cataclysm* fits him better after this morning."

"Well, I hope he catches thousands of mice for you."

"Well, *I* hope there aren't thousands of mice in my lodgings!" He reached down and ruffled her hair, an odd smile on his face. "Anyway, it was worth it to hear you give that sanctimonious old windbag such a trimming."

CHAPTER NINE

It wasn't very late in the afternoon when a messenger arrived from the Dean to escort Alice to an audience with Father Boyce. Her heart was beating uncomfortably hard when the messenger stopped before a heavy door on the second floor of the Deanery and tapped lightly.

"Yes."

The messenger swung the door open, then stood aside for Alice to enter. She did, then stopped. It was an imposing chamber, paneled with dark wood and lavishly carpeted. There was an elaborate brass and crystal chandelier hanging from the ceiling, and the Dean was seated behind an enormous table, silhouetted against the arched leaded glass windows behind him. Alice took a deep breath, made a small bow, and walked resolutely across what seemed a vast expanse of carpet to stand before the Dean's table. For a moment, they studied each other in silence. The Very Reverend Edgar Boyce, Dean of York Minster, was a lean, handsome man with an imposing mane of white hair, keen hazel eyes and a hint of wry humor about his mouth.

"Well, young man," he begun at last, "what is it they call you — Pup?"

"Yes, Father."

"I've heard Father Cooper's version of the story. Suppose you tell me yours."

Alice lifted her chin and related the entire story of Catechism in a clear, steady voice. "And when I heard him prating on and on about propriety and reverence and so on, it made me so angry that I lost my temper. I called him a hypocrite, and when he said he'd report my insolence to you, I told him I didn't care and called him a fat hypocrite," she ended a little defiantly.

The Dean knit his brow. "Why did it make you so angry for him to talk of propriety?" he asked.

"He's a fine one to talk about propriety!" she retorted. "He went on and *on* about how awful it was for me to keep Cathechism in the cathedral, when *he's* using the cathedral to meet secretly with —" She stopped, appalled. She hadn't meant to say that. Now what was she to do?

The Dean regarded her sternly. "To meet secretly with whom?" he prompted.

"Well, that's the trouble, Father. I don't really know." She was thinking frantically. "I overheard — by accident — Father Cooper talking with someone. I didn't understand it completely, but it sounded very, well, shady. He said something about buying someone's silence — or corroboration. It didn't sound like the proper attitude for a priest."

The Dean shook his head. "That's rather thin." Then he sat back and studied Alice, as though waiting for something. She shifted uncomfortably but held his gaze.

"I think," the Dean said finally, "you had better tell me the whole tale, Pup."

"It didn't make much sense to me," she temporized, "but I'll tell you all I remember. The first man said something like 'the peasants are agog with it,' and Father Cooper said —"

"How did you know it was Father Cooper? Did you see his face?"

"No, Father, but his voice is rather distinctive."

"Well, go on."

"Father Cooper said something like 'Peasants are peasants. You needn't bother about them.' And he mentioned something about keeping a child shut away. And the other man said, 'You mean, tell people the child is mad? But the governess . . .' And then Father Cooper said his bit about buying silence or corroboration. Then they lowered their voices, and I could only hear bits and snatches. Father Cooper said something about disposing of someone and someone else mentioned France, but I couldn't make anything out of it."

The Dean laced his fingers together and studied them for a moment; then he looked up at Alice. "What an imagination you have, Pup. There's probably a perfectly innocent explanation." He paused. "Now, if you will apologize to Father Cooper, we will consider the matter closed."

Alice's chin jutted rebelliously. "But I'm not sorry! He *is* a fat hypocrite!"

"And *you* are an impertinent little boy," the Dean replied grimly. "You will do as I say."

She looked up into his stern, closed face and realized it would be worse than useless to argue. She bowed her head. "Yes, Father Boyce."

"If you can't in conscience tell him you are sorry for what you said," the Dean added in a rather gentler tone, "then apologize for having lost your temper."

"Yes, Father."

"By the way, what have you done with the kitten?"

"Master Kenton offered to take it in," she told him.

His eyes widened. "Kenton?"

She nodded. "He said it could take care of the mice in his lodgings."

"Mice," he repeated; amusement quivered on his lips. "I see. Well, run along now, Pup, but don't forget to speak to Father Cooper."

"Yes, Father Boyce," she murmured and, with a small bow, took herself off.

The Dean watched her go speculatively; as the door closed, he shook his head. "Kenton," he repeated. "Who'd have thought it?"

The days settled back to their usual routine. Father Cooper had to content himself with Alice's carefully worded apology, and although he was far from pacified, they had a tacit agreement to stay as far out of each other's way as possible. Preparations for the Christmas Eve service were well under way in the choir, and Alice was surprised and delighted by the large variety of pieces they were doing. As Advent went on, more and more of the boys began to discuss what they would do over their winter recess, for they were on vacation from the day after Christmas until the first Sunday after Epiphany — sixteen whole days! Most of the boys would go home; but in the winter traveling was difficult, so the boys who lived far away stayed at the school. Alice was not at all troubled that she would have to stay, too. Geoffrey and his grandmother had promised to put her up if things got too dull; Randall and Nate lived in York, so they would be nearby; and Orlando thought he would be staying at the school as well.

One morning, Alice woke to find snow falling — not the limp, wet-feathers stuff they had in London, but light, sparkling snow that stayed on the streets and rooftops and blew about in the wind. She dressed and did her chores more quickly than usual, and instead of taking time to eat the Dame's bread and cheese, she simply tumbled it into a napkin and tucked it in her pocket. She went out into the eddying snow.

When she arrived at the choir room, she lit a candle and set it next to the music rack. She rubbed her hands together, trying to warm them a little, then began with her scales. She had been practicing for a while when, quite suddenly, she knew she was no longer alone.

Turning quickly, she found Masters Frost and Kenton standing in the doorway. She jumped up.

"I'm sorry. I didn't know you wanted to use the room."

"Relax, Pup," Master Kenton advised. "We were looking for you."

"For me?" she echoed. "I'm not in trouble again, am I?"

"Nothing like that," Master Frost assured her. "Pup, we have a piece we'd like you to read. If it works, we'll use it on Christmas Eve. It's a setting of a very lovely text from the eleventh chapter of the book of Isaiah. Here." He gave her some sheets of music. "Shall we try it?"

"I'm not warmed up," Alice said.

"We'll make allowances," Master Kenton said as he took his place at the keyboard. "Ready?"

She nodded and looked down at the music; it was written in Master Kenton's unmistakable hand. *And there shall come forth a rod out of the stem of Jesse . . .* Kenton played the short introduction and Alice began to sing. The music was hauntingly sweet. The twining of the voice with the accompaniment was so skillfully done that it seemed completely free. *The wolf also shall dwell with the lamb, and the leopard shall lie down with the kid . . . and a little child shall lead them.* The music, built gently, growing from sweetness through beauty to the final statement. *For the earth shall be full of the knowledge of the Lord as the waters cover the sea.* Alice listened to the sound die away, filled with awe at the incredible power of the music. As the silence thickened around them, she raised her eyes to Master Kenton's face; she knew that he had composed this wonderful music.

"What a beautiful piece," she said softly.

"Yes, indeed," Master Frost agreed. "We *will* use it on Christmas Eve. You'll have to sing it from the organ loft, but we can work that out later on. Now, I must go find those copies of 'Ding, Dong Merrily.' Thank you both," he called over his shoulder as he went out.

"Are you still wondering how such a sour old man can write such music?" Master Kenton asked wryly.

"No, sir. I'm wondering how *anyone* can. My father would —" She stopped herself in time, biting her lips together. Then she sighed and shook her head. "— would never have understood." Master Kenton looked at her questioningly, but before he could speak she said, in as normal a tone as she could manage, "But there's a section or two I'm pretty shaky on."

"More than two, Pup."

She grinned. "Well, yes. Will you go over them with me?"

When Master Frost returned a few minutes later, they were hard at work. He watched from the doorway for a moment, then slipped out again. Later, he interrupted them to say it was nearly time for Matins.

Three days before Christmas, the choristers were given

a day off from their classes to go out into the woods to cut the boughs that would decorate the cathedral.

"We do it every year," Randall told Alice as they walked along the snowy road behind one of the two sledges. "Holly and pine boughs. And then tomorrow we put them up all over the cathedral — the smell is really wonderful, especially with the frankincense. After the cathedral is all decorated, the Dean always has us up to the Deanery and gives us hot spiced cider and little cakes."

"Oh, stop!" She laughed. "You're making me hungry."

"Hey, Pup," Geoffrey called.

She turned, then dodged, for Geoffrey had lobbed a snowball in her direction. Bending quickly, she scooped up some snow, packed it, and tossed it at Geoffrey. She missed but instead struck Nate, who was walking nearby. In a moment, the expedition was transformed into a free-for-all that lasted until the horse pulling the first sledge was struck; then Emery and the other supervisors put a forceful stop to the snow battle.

The forest was beautiful. It was a bright, cold day, and the winter sun cast blue shadows on the snow. They took small saws from the sledges and set off into the trees.

"Now don't go too far," Emery advised. "There's plenty close to hand."

They made merry work of it. Alice caught Geoffrey beneath a snow-laden fir branch and, with a deft shake, sent a shower of snow over his head; he chased her through the woods until she caught up with Randall and tried to hide behind him.

"Save me," she gasped, laughing.

Randall grinned. " How'd you get so snowy, Geoffrey?"

"That Pup! Help me get my hands on him!"

Randall shook a reproving finger at them both. "You should be gathering holly, not chasing each other through the snow," he said primly.

Geoffrey and Alice exchanged looks, then both leaped at Randall and rolled him over and over in the snow. Nate came up to see what was going on; a moment later Orlando appeared to find Randall sprawled on his back with Geoffrey and Nate holding him down while Alice posed, like a conquering hero, with her foot on his chest.

"Stop laughing, Orlando, and get them off me!" Randall pleaded.

Orlando was happy to oblige. A few minutes later Emery came over to them, hiding a smile at their antics.

"When you have worked off your exuberance, you could apply yourselves to the task at hand," he suggested mildly.

A moment later, with saintly expressions on their faces, they were busily gathering boughs and piling them on the sledges until they were full; then they started back. Alice fixed a spray of holly to each of the horses' bridles and patted their noses. Several boys took up branches and swung them about. Someone began a carol, and by the time they reached the city gates, the choristers had sorted themselves into an impromptu procession, singing in their clear, high voices. When they reached the cathedral, the sledges pulled up to the great west doors. They unloaded quickly, then carried the boughs inside, heaping the greens in two piles at the back of the nave. As soon as the unloading was done they sprinted home. There was barely time to change out of their wet things before Evensong.

"I've never had such fun," Alice confided to Orlando as they hurried back to the cathedral.

"Wait until Christmas morning," he told her. "We all gather in the choir room after the service and have a little party. It's lots of fun. Ol' Bennett brings a tray of little cakes with Latin verbs on them, and you get to eat the ones you can translate. And he never puts hard ones on! Last year, Master Benbowe and Emery brought enough candy to feed an army, and old Frost gave each of us a ha'penny. And we exchange gifts and —"

"Gifts!" she interrupted, dismayed. "But Orlando, I didn't know! I haven't got anything for anyone." And no money, either, she added silently.

Orlando shrugged. "Don't worry about it, Pup. It's bound to work out. My first year, my father forgot to send me any spending money. I told the Dame all about it, and — if you can believe it — she helped me bake gingerbread men — enough for everyone. We tied little bows of red yarn around their necks to make them look festive." He broke off as they reached the organ loft and began rummaging in the closet for their cassocks and surplices.

"Hurry along!" Master Frost urged from his place. "We're running late."

When the boys started home after the service, Alice told them not to wait for her. She had to talk to Master Kenton. She went and stood by the organ while he changed his shoes.

"Master Kenton," she began tentatively, "what do you want for Christmas?"

For a long moment Kenton simply stared at her. Then he shrugged and went back to changing his shoes. "Peace and quiet and a long vacation," he said lightly, without looking up.

She pondered. "If you taught me to play the organ, you could have a vacation."

"Now, there's a thought." He studied her speculatively. "No good. You're too short. Your feet won't reach the pedal board. Besides, it would take too long. Did you want something, Pup?"

"N-no."

"Then I'll be off. I'm meeting an old friend for dinner — an old friend of yours, in fact — William Hunnis."

"O-oh," she gasped, then recovered herself. "What's he doing in York?"

Master Kenton shrugged. "I don't know. I guess he'll tell me over dinner. Perhaps he'll come around tomorrow to see you. Shall I suggest it?"

"Yes. Yes, do. And greet him for me, sir."

"Of course. Goodnight, Pup." He swept up his music and made for the stairway.

"Goodnight, sir," she said after him. Then she sat down and cradled her head in her hands. This was awful — *worse* than awful — for either Master Hunnis would deny any knowledge of an Alister Tucker, and Master Kenton would think her a liar, or he would figure out the truth and tell him and she would be punished and sent away. She fought back tears, then realized she'd better get home to her supper. She made her way slowly to the stairs and then down. When she went out into the nave, she saw a tall figure standing there. In the faint light it was hard to make out his features, but there was something unmistakable about the way he held himself.

"I thought that was your voice," he said quietly. "My poor child!"

"Master Hunnis!" She threw herself at him and gave him a fierce hug. "What are you doing here?"

"Your Master Kenton wrote to me. He wanted to know all about some fellow named Alister Tucker, a former student of mine. I thought it might be you."

"Yes. Oh, but please, Master Hunnis, please don't tell them about me. They all think I'm a boy."

Master Frost, who had been coming quietly up the north aisle with a sheaf of music under one arm, stopped short in amazement.

Master Hunnis sighed. "Let me walk you home."

"Yes, of course," she replied, slipping her hand confidingly into his.

When Master Frost heard the door shut behind them, he let out his breath in a long, shuddering gasp. "Merciful heavens," he said aloud. "Pup is a girl? Now what am I going to do about that?"

CHAPTER TEN

Outside in the clear, cold night, Alice and Master Hunnis started toward Dame Agnes's.

"Do you like it here?" he asked her. "Do they treat you well?"

"Yes. Oh yes. I'm learning all sorts of interesting things at the school — Latin, even — and Master Kenton is teaching me to play the virginal."

"Is he? Hugh? Well, well. That's wonderful, child. He's a fine musician."

She looked up into Master Hunnis's face. "You won't tell, will you? Promise?"

He stopped walking, studying the small, hopeful face turned up to him. "Alice," he said softly, "what really happened to your father?"

She swallowed hard. "Murdered," she whispered. "And by the Queen's orders."

"By the Queen's orders? Are you sure? But Alice —"

"I *heard* the murderers say that the Queen would be pleased," she interrupted, her voice tight.

"Who are they, Alice? Do you know them?"

She lowered her voice still further. "Lord Crofton and Sir Roderick Donne."

He whistled softly. "Speak to the Dean, Alice. He'd shield you."

"From the Queen?" she demanded. "How could he?"

"I can't believe the Queen is involved, but even if she were, she won't want revenge against *you*. You aren't involved in any of your father's indiscretions."

Alice thought of Father Cooper and the other conspirators and shivered. "But they'd send me away. Please don't tell, Master."

"I should," he said, looking down at her. "I ought to take you straight to the Dean and consign you to his care. Alice, Alice, wouldn't that be better?"

Tears sprang to her eyes; she pressed her lips together. Much as she wanted to believe the Dean could keep her safe, the thought of Father Cooper daunted her. It would be so much easier for him if he knew where she was; and she was afraid she could never convince the Dean that his own Sub-Dean was involved in a murder. Besides, the Dean could hardly keep her in his palace; he would have to send her away somewhere. She swallowed hard. She had no family left; she would be sent to strangers. She had lost so much already, she couldn't face the possibility of losing her friends here as well. She looked up at Master Hunnis and shook her head.

He sighed. "Tell me. How did you hit on the notion of the cathedral choir?"

She managed a wan smile. "I didn't hit on it — they hit on me. One of the boys bumped into me on the street by accident and knocked me down. After that, they sort of adopted me. It was Geoffrey's idea that I dress up as a choirboy and try to pass unnoticed in the choir."

"Do you mean to tell me all the boys know you're a girl?" he demanded incredulously.

"Not all of them, just some of the older ones. Frankly, it would be very awkward if they didn't know, but as it is, they've arranged for me to have a private alcove in which to wash and dress."

"And does anyone else know? Kenton or Frost?"

"No! Master Hunnis, I think they'd be frightfully angry. They'd—" Her voice caught. "They'd send me away. I couldn't bear it. Please don't tell them."

"Alice, child," he said after a long pause, "they are bound to find out eventually. Someone will make a slip — with so many in on the secret, I'm surprised it hasn't happened already. Wouldn't it be better to tell them rather than to let them find out? Perhaps they wouldn't be so angry, then."

"But they'd *never* let me stay," she said forlornly. "And I wouldn't be able to study with Kenton or Barnstable or to sing in the choir."

He was silent. Finally, he sighed heavily. "I wish I knew what was right, Alice. In truth, if Donne and Crofton are looking for you, they'd never think of looking here. Perhaps you *are* safer posing as a boy for a while. Alice, I'll bargain with you. I'll keep your secret on one condition: let me speak to the Queen when I return to London."

"But —"

"Alice, Her Majesty *liked* your father. She would never have ordered him murdered." He looked into her troubled eyes. "Trust me."

She took a deep breath and nodded. "And you'll keep my secret?"

"Yes, I promise. Adrian will probably want my head on Traitor's Gate when he finds out — and Hugh, too — but I'll be in London." He started to walk again rather slowly. "Promise me, child, when they find out you're a girl, for the love of heaven, tell them who you are and *make* the Dean listen to you."

"He might not believe me."

"You must make him believe you. And now, child, I must hurry. Kenton will be waiting for me. Quickly, tell me what you've told people about your background. He'll want to know."

"I'm an only child. My father is dead of plague, and my mother died when I was small. My father felt that music was frivolous and —"

"Poor, maligned Henry," Hunnis said, shaking his head.

"Well, what was I to say when Master Barnstable asked me why, in the name of God, wasn't I in the Chapel Royal? I told him you and my father were old friends and that, as a special favor to him, you had agreed not to let me in — on the condition that he allow you to teach me to sing."

"You told *Barnstable* that?" Master Hunnis asked weakly. He sighed. "Alas for my reputation."

"Well, I'm sorry, but what was I to say? Anyway, I think that's about all. I've been pretty reticent."

"Thank heaven for small favors," he said, nodding. "It's enough. I'll embroider it a little, a *very* little. I'll come around to see you tomorrow — Hugh is bound to suggest it. I'd like to hear you sing — and play. And I'll need to fill you in on the details of your life." He smiled a little oddly, then reached into his pocket, pulled something out, and pressed it into her hand. "Take that from me. Call it a Christmas present, if you like. Is this where you live?" he asked as she stopped at the kitchen door. "Goodnight then, child."

"Goodnight, Master Hunnis. And — and thank you," she whispered. She gave him a quick hug, then pulled the door open and slipped inside. It wasn't until she was undressing for bed that she had a chance to examine Hunnis's gift. It was a small purse containing one shilling and twelve pence; it seemed a fortune. Silently, she blessed him as she slipped the purse under her pillow and climbed into bed.

"There you are, Hunnis. I'd almost given you up," Kenton said in greeting. He rose and the two men shooks hands; they both sat down at the table and Kenton looked around for the innkeeper. The man appeared almost magically, quickly produced two tankards of ale, and assured them their dinners would be ready in a twinkling. After he'd gone, Kenton and Hunnis sat for a moment, silently studying each other. Hunnis was tall and thin, with gentle, gray eyes set in a narrow face furrowed with wrinkles.

"So how have you been?" asked Kenton. "And what brings you to York?"

"I'm well enough for an old man," he said dryly. "My sister asked me to spend Christmas with her, so I decided I'd let Crane do the Christmas services without me for once. It's bound to be good for him. You know, Hugh, it isn't going to be too many more years before I retire. The Chapel Royal is such a large responsibility."

Kenton smiled sardonically. "You know you love it, William."

"But there are so many *details* to see to," he began, then broke off with a rueful smile. "You know me too well. But tell me about Alister. Is he working hard for you?"

Before Kenton could answer, their food arrived, and for the next few minutes both men were too busy eating to spare much effort for conversation.

"This is very good," Kenton said at last. "Yes, Pup — as we call him — is working *very* hard. But tell me, William — you taught him — why the devil didn't you tap him for the Chapel Royal? He has a remarkable voice."

Hunnis shifted uncomfortably. "It was in the nature of a special favor for Alister's father. Andrew was set on having his son go into the law, and he was afraid to encourage his musical talents for fear he'd pursue them instead. Andrew always felt that music was, oh, frivolous, I suppose — an unworthy occupation for any son of his."

"That's foolishness!" Kenton snapped. "And you were party to it? I'm surprised at you."

"Andrew was a very old friend, and Alister was his only son. I couldn't go against him. Besides, I thought that Andrew might become reconciled to it when he saw how gifted the boy was if I didn't anger him too much."

Kenton was silent for a moment, a slight scowl on his face. "You're not going to take the boy now for the Chapel Royal, are you?"

Hunnis shook his head. "I couldn't." A faint smile lit his eyes. "Adrian would never forgive me."

"That's true enough," Kenton replied with an answering glimmer.

"Is someone teaching Alister the virginal? He always wanted to learn."

"I'm teaching him. He's —"

"*You've* taken him on? I thought you didn't like to teach children."

Kenton shrugged. "As a general rule I don't, but Pup's different. He's extremely talented, as you know, and he *works*. Why don't you come around tomorrow? Then you can hear him sing and play. He's making great strides, and he's miles ahead of even the advanced group in Theory. You taught him well, William."

Hunnis bowed slightly, then smiled. "I will come around tomorrow, then, before I leave."

"You aren't spending Christmas in York?"

He shook his head. "My sister and her husband live in Kirbymoorside. But I trust I'll have a chance to see Adrian tomorrow. It's been a long time." He turned his head and caught the innkeeper's eye. "May we have some more ale, please?"

"A good rehearsal," Master Frost told his choir the next morning as he prepared to dismiss them. "There are no classes this afternoon" — there were muffled cheers — "so that you will all be free to decorate the cathedral. And of course, afterward there is the Dean's tea."

"Tea?" Geoffrey whispered to Alice. "It's more like a feast. Just wait."

"Tomorrow," Master Frost went on, "we'll be rehearsing in the cathedral, so we'll meet there after breakfast." He stopped and the choir got up to go. "Pup, can you stay for a few minutes?" he asked.

She nodded, then turned to Geoffrey. "Will you tell the Dame I won't be there for lunch, please? My old teacher, Master Hunnis, is here, and I want to visit with him."

"Sure," Geoffrey agreed cheerfully. "Shall I save you something, or do you think he's good for a meal?"

"I don't think you need to bother, thanks anyway. There's the Dean's tea, after all."

"Right you are." He raised a hand in a casual salute and left with the others.

Hunnis, who had been sitting in the back of the choir room during the rehearsal, came forward as Frost and Kenton approached Alice.

"We need to check the balance between you and the organ for your solo," Master Frost said, "and since William wants to hear you sing, we thought this would be an ideal time."

In the space of a few minutes, Alice and Kenton had taken their places in the organ loft. Both Frost and Hunnis had decided to stay in the nave in order to listen.

"You stand here," Master Kenton instructed her, "so I can see you. Tomorrow night, you'll have a candle-stand beside you — I'll see the verger about it — so you'll have enough light. Ready?"

At her nod, he began. It took him a minute or two to find a combination of stops that pleased him, then they went through the piece. When they finished, Master Frost came upstairs.

"The balance is fine — that's going to be just lovely tomorrow. Are you comfortable with it, Pup?"

"Yes, sir."

"Good. Then that's all we need. Thank you. Master Hunnis is waiting for you downstairs."

"See you later, scamp," Kenton added as she started downstairs.

Master Hunnis was waiting by the door. "How beautiful," he said quietly. "That's Hugh's — Master Kenton's — work, isn't it?"

"Yes."

"I'd still like to hear you play. Do you suppose the choir room is free?"

She nodded and led the way back. She played a couple of delicate dances for him, and he told her he was amazed at her progress.

"I wish I had longer with you, child, but I need to set out soon if I'm going to be at my sister's by night-fall. Why don't you come with me into the market-place? I'll buy you a meat pasty or something."

Alice agreed readily, and in a short while they were threading their way through the crowds of people and the tangle of booths and stalls. Vendors huddled be-side their braziers and tried to outshout each other: Fish, fresh fish! Sweet cakes and comfits! Fine teas! Hot meat pies! Master Hunnis led her unerringly to the stall where meat pies were sold, and a moment later they had both retreated into a doorway out of the rush to eat their lunch. The pies were good, hot and spicy, though rather messy. When they had finished, Hunnis sighed and smiled a little sadly.

"I must go. I'm not one for drawn-out farewells. I'll write to you after I've spoken to the Queen to let you know what I've learned. In the meantime, take care of yourself. If you find you need me, I'm in Kirbymoor-side through Christmas, and after that I'll be back at the Chapel Royal in London."

"Thank you, Master, for everything." She swallowed hard, willing her voice not to quaver. "Good-bye." She hugged him.

"Good-bye," he murmured, then he left the doorway and was soon lost in the crowd. For a moment, Alice stood watching him.

"Don't waste time!" she told herself sternly. "There's none to spare." She set off into the eddying crowds, searching for the herb seller's booth.

She found it, a drab, gray stall amongst the garishly painted ones. There were bunches of dried plants tied up with twine and hanging from the ceiling, and many small jars with curious labels lined the shelves on the wall. The vendor himself was a wizened old man, hunched over a brazier full of glowing coals. He looked up as she stopped at his booth, regarding her with pale, rheumy eyes before he rose stiffly to his feet.

"Do you have any catnip, sir?"

"Ah." His voice was wispy and thin. *"Napeta cataria.* Also called catmint. To cure a colic or charm a cat . . ." He bent slowly and looked on one of the lower shelves. A moment later he produced two large packets. "Half-pence for two."

Alice gave him the coin and tucked the packets into her pockets. For a time she wandered aimlessly, enjoying the noise and the bustle. Somewhat to her surprise, she found herself in front of a candy seller's booth. There were trays and trays of delicious-looking candies, but what caught Alice's eyes were exquisite little animals fashioned out of marzipan. She counted quickly in her head, then turned to the motherly looking woman behind the counter.

"If I wanted three dozen of those" — she gestured to the animals — "how much would that cost?"

The woman smiled. "Ordinarily, it'd be sixpence, but since it's so near Christmas, I'd give them to you for four."

Alice fished in her purse and produced the coins. "Then that's what I'd like, please."

Taking the coins, the woman deftly packaged the three dozen animals. She tied the parcel with a piece of red twine and gave it to Alice. "A Merry Christmas to you, young sir."

"Thank you. The same to you and yours," she replied as she set off again. All she had to do was to find something for Master Kenton. But what? She wished she'd thought to ask Master Hunnis what Kenton might like.

She wandered through the stalls, pausing briefly at a bookseller's and a tea dealer's, but the books were quite expensive and she didn't know what sort of tea he liked. Time was getting short, too. She was about to give up and go back when she saw it, hanging up in a weaver's stall: a rich, mulberry red muffler. She remembered the drab one he usually wore and smiled. She went over to the weaver's to examine it. The muffler was woven of fine, soft wool; it felt very thick and warm and had a silky fringe on each end. She was a little daunted to find the weaver wanted a whole shilling for it, but she hesitated only a moment. He would be sure to like it; it was perfect. She put the coin on the counter and waited while the weaver wrapped it for her. With her purchases under her arms, she hurried back to the dormitory. As she had hoped, no one was there. She ran upstairs and pushed the parcels under her bed. Then she went briskly off to the cathedral.

Decorating the cathedral took surprisingly little time, for not only were the choirboys there but most of the other choir men, and several of the masters were also helping. At one point, Alice slipped away with several sprigs of holly and some bright berries. She ran up to the organ loft, climbed carefully up on the organ bench, and tied the holly to the music rack. Then she rejoined the others.

When the decorating was finished, they all went over to the Deanery, where they were ceremoniously ushered into an enormous downstairs parlor by two liveried footmen. A long trestle table held a large number of silver platters and trays, all with interesting things to eat arranged on them. In the middle of the table stood a huge pewter punch bowl and several rows of cut glass cups. As they admired the lavish table, a maid entered carrying a great kettle full of steaming liquid and emptied it into the punch bowl. One of the footmen took his place behind the punch bowl and began deftly filling cups. Alice's mouth began to water at the sweet, pungent fragrance filtering toward her. Beside her, Orlando groaned softly.

"Hungry?" she asked him.

"I could eat a bishop — miter and all!" he whispered.

At that moment, the Dean entered. He greeted them all with a smile and a nod, then bowed his head and gave a simple blessing.

"Amen," Alice murmured, then joined the others

as they surged discreetly toward the table. Her plate filled, she found a place to stand, comfortably near the fire, and was enjoying the dainty pastries and the lovely, hot spiced cider when Geoffrey joined her.

"I love Christmas," he said. "It's better than any other holiday. Gram always cooks a big goose and makes plum pudding. I can't wait."

"You'll have to, Geoffrey," Alice pointed out.

He made a face. "Don't you ever get tired of being so *practical?*"

She grinned back. "To tell the truth, I can hardly wait myself. Orlando told me there's a party and everything." A wistful look came into her eyes. "We never made much of Christmas at home. Father was too busy. Anne would cook a goose, and if I was lucky I could watch some of the revelry the servants had belowstairs. I used to try to get my father to take me to the Chapel Royal services, but he didn't really like to go. One year he told me" — she imitated his voice and manner — " 'I've better things to do than listen to the demented gibberings of a senile reprobate in clerical garb — and so I told Bishop Anscott to his face.' " As she looked up at Geoffrey, she caught sight of Father Cooper standing just behind him; his hand was frozen motionless halfway between his plate and his mouth, and he was staring at Alice intently. She felt the expression drain out of her face as she stared back at him, remembering too late the stir her father had caused by insulting Bishop Anscott. Then Father Cooper blinked and smiled at her, a curiously triumphant smile.

"Merry Christmas, ah, Alister. Merry Christmas," he said. She wondered if she'd imagined the emphasis on the first two syllables of her name. She pulled herself together and forced a smile.

"Merry Christmas, Father Cooper."

"Looking forward to the celebrations are you, ah, Alister?"

"Oh yes, Father."

He nodded jovially and turned back toward the refreshment table. Alice watched him go with troubled eyes. She looked up to see Master Kenton watching her from across the room, a faint frown on his face. Hurriedly she turned back to Geoffrey.

"Have you tried these?" she asked, indicating a delicate shell of pastry filled with a sweet, creamy mixture of fruit. "They're really good."

He nodded. For a moment he looked as though he were going to ask awkward questions, but he changed his mind, and they talked casually until Master Frost announced that it was time for the Evensong rehearsal.

The candles and firelight gleamed cheerfully on the silver tea service. Father Cooper dismissed the servant with a wave of his hand and beamed at his two visitors.

"I'm *so* glad you've come, gentlemen. And such a surprise. I wasn't expecting you until after Christmas."

"Oh, stop it, Dunstan," Sir Roderick snapped. "If you really must know, things are cursed uncomfortable at Court! Queen Elizabeth is furious that one of her pet musicians has been killed, and under — how does she put it? — such *peculiar* circumstances. You told us she'd be pleased to have Sir Henry out of the way!"

"And how was I to guess she'd value his music so highly? My God, the man's a suspected Papist! A *sensible* ruler would be dancing with joy at his untimely end." Father Cooper felt a surge of anger. It wasn't fair! It had been such a good plan. Sir Henry Tuckfield didn't have any heirs, just that wretched girl, and his earldom was entailed. With his death, his lands would revert to the Crown, and a grateful Queen would have given them all preferment. He knew Donne and Crofton both craved Court appointments, and while the Queen couldn't have given him outright the bishopric he coveted, her word would carry weight in the councils of the Church.

"All right, Dunstan," Lord Crofton replied irritably. "We're not blaming you. But what are we going to do? Right now, Elizabeth hasn't any proof it wasn't an accident, but *where the devil is the girl?* She must know something or she'd have surfaced."

"Obviously," Father Cooper replied, mildly contemptuous. "What a pair of conspirators you are — foiled by a girl-child not even twelve years old. Why, you must find her and silence her."

"That's a fine thing for you to say, Dunstan," Sir Roderick retorted. "It was supposed to be your lookout to find the brat."

"Time and again I must save your bacon," he said, affecting weariness. "I have found the child — or at least I think so." He held up a hand to still their questions. "Do you remember what it was Henry Tuckfield said to Bishop Anscott?"

"I fail to see —" Lord Crofton began stiffly, but Sir Roderick interrupted, laughing.

"Lord, yes! Something about 'the demented gibberings of a senile reprobate in clerical garb.' It was the talk of the Court for weeks. Why?"

"I overheard someone quoting that — in a very passable imitation of Henry Tuckfield's voice — and ascribing it to 'Father.' "

"Where?" Lord Croften burst out. "I'll —"

"Patience," Father Cooper cautioned. "These things must be carefully planned. They require finesse. Besides, I'm not perfectly certain it *is* Alice Tuckfield, as I've never seen her before. You'll both have to help identify her, and toward that end you must go to the midnight service tomorrow."

"Dunstan, will you stop being so cryptic," Lord Crofton demanded irritably, "and come to the point?"

"Unless I am very much mistaken," he stated grandly, "Alice Tuckfield is in the choir."

CHAPTER ELEVEN

"Now," Master Frost told them when they gathered in the cathedral for the morning rehearsal, "we're going to go straight through the service in order. The only things that will be missing are the lessons and the prayers. Pup, your piece will be the first thing after the opening prayer, so you can go right up to the organ loft now and stay there through the introit and the processional. Master Kenton needs someone to turn pages and pull stops. When you're done, come and join the left-hand side of the choir as discreetly as you can. Understand?"

She nodded.

"Then go with Master Kenton. He'll tell you what he wants you to do."

Alice had to run a little to keep up with Master Kenton's long strides. When they reached the organ loft, he sat down on the bench and arranged some music on the rack.

"Come here," he said, pointing to where he wanted her to stand. "Can you reach to turn my pages? Good. When I get to here" — he pointed to a place on the third page — "I want you to pull out these stops." He indicated a cluster of stops. She read their odd names. BOURDON. CHIMNEY FLUTE. NIGHT HORN. "Pull them out together," he instructed, "like this. Use both hands. Fine. Right after you turn the third page, come around in back of me to the other side — right — and as soon as I get to here" — he pointed to a rest — "pull out this — quickly. You only have a beat." SWELL TO GREAT, she read. "Then turn my last page and you're done. Have you got that?"

"I think so."

"We'll soon see." He pulled out several stops and began to play. "That will work," he told her as the choir sang the introit and he opened his hymnal to the processional hymn. "Just don't catch your surplice on fire with the candles."

When, a little while later, Alice slipped into her place in the front row of the choir, she found herself next to Orlando. He rolled his eyes expressively.

"What a piece! You sound like an angel. Will you be nervous tonight?"

"I don't know. Probably." She smiled ruefully. "But I know I'll be petrified pulling stops for Master Kenton. What if I make a mistake?"

"He'll flay you," Orlando told her cheerfully.

"You're a great comfort," she retorted before they both had to stop talking to sing.

"The trio is next," Master Frost said when they were through perhaps half of the music. "Can you sing from your places?" He sounded doubtful even as he asked, for Emery and Alice were on one side of the choir and Christopher was in the back of the other side. When they tried it, he stopped them before they were halfway through the first page. He shook his head. "You'll have to sing from the organ loft. During the lesson before your piece" — he consulted a sheet on his music stand — " 'And there were in the same country shepherds,' you three sneak out and go up to the organ loft."

When they had taken their places in the organ loft, Kenton gave discreet pitches and they began. Afterward, they slipped unobtrusively back to their seats, and the rest of the rehearsal passed quickly.

"The Christmas Eve service begins at midnight," Master Frost told them. "I want you all in the choir room, in your cassocks and surplices, no later than quarter past eleven. We'll have a brief warmup and go over some last-minute things. Boys, if you can possibly manage it, please get some rest this afternoon — you can't sing if you're falling asleep. Now, go along to your lunches. Don't forget: Evensong as usual."

As the choir left, Master Frost followed Alice with his eyes, a frown creasing his brow.

"Something on your mind?" Master Kenton asked sardonically.

Master Frost jumped. "No, no. Why do you ask?"

"You don't have to tell me, you know, but you don't

usually frown like that unless something's bothering you."

The choirmaster sighed. "It's Pup," he began, then hesitated. "I, well, he has quite a large role in tonight's service, and I don't even know if he gets nervous. We've never heard him perform in public. What if he clutches?"

Kenton shrugged. "If he clutches, I'm a trout. Don't worry yourself, Adrian."

At a few minutes after eleven that night, Alice arrived in the choir room with her cassock and surplice draped over her arm. Many of the choir members were already there, talking quietly. She put on her cassock and buttoned it, then struggled into her surplice.

"Hold still." It was Master Kenton's voice. She froze obediently while he twitched the white garment straight. "That's better. Are you nervous, Pup?"

"Not yet, except about pulling stops," she confessed. "I'm terrified I'll botch it and you'll strangle me. Who usually does it for you, sir?"

He shrugged. "Master Frost. Emery used to sometimes until the time he pulled out the REGAL instead of the BOURDON. I wasn't very nice about it."

"I'll bet you weren't! But he, at least, is nearer your size."

He looked down at her, raising an eyebrow. "You don't think I'd offer you violence?"

"I don't think it, sir," she retorted, "I know it!"

Just then Master Frost entered, carrying a crate full

of candles, and conversation stopped. He looked around the room.

"One of the last-minute things I forgot to mention was the candles for the recessional. Everyone be sure to take one as we leave to go over to the cathedral. There will be two large candles in stands, one on either side of the choir. At the end of the service, as the lines file off during the last hymn, each of you will light your candle before you start up the center of the nave. Is that clear? Good. Let's warm up."

In what seemed a very short time, the choir was gathered in the south transept while Alice and Master Kenton went up to the organ loft. The cathedral was filled with people; not only were there no empty seats, but people were standing between the columns and even overflowing into the aisles.

"Here we go," Master Kenton said as he pulled out some stops and Alice took her place on his left. "Do you remember what to do?"

She managed a smile. "I devoutly trust so."

Kenton nodded, then began to play. Alice took a deep breath, bit her lip, and rapidly reviewed the instructions in her mind. She knew Master Kenton was playing very well, but she dared not relax into the music; she held herself a little aloof, concentrating hard on what she needed to do. When the prelude was over, Kenton looked over at her and smiled. She sat down on one of the benches in the back row while the choir sang the introit. Then came the processional hymn. It felt odd to be standing still instead of marching with the rest of the choir, and though she knew she was singing, all she could hear was the organ. The bass notes of the pedal seemed to set her vibrating, as if she were a string in a great harp. Below, she could see the procession: thurifer, crucifer, acolytes, choir, priests, Dean, Archbishop. The candlelight gleamed on the great gold cross, touched the surplices of the choir, and set the jewels in the Archbishop's miter blazing with their own fire. When the choir had taken its place before the hymn was finished, she gathered up her music and went to stand between the organ and the tall candlestand; she didn't know how long the opening prayer would be.

". . . In the name of the Father, the Son, and the Holy Ghost, Amen."

She looked over at Master Kenton and nodded slightly. He began, and for an instant she felt a flash of panic, but a deep breath steadied her and she came in without even a hint of a quaver. As she sang, she lost all sense of anything but the music; she felt unimportant, a vessel, only, from which the music emptied itself. And when the music had dissipated, leaving behind it an awed hush, it took her a moment to recollect herself. Kenton leaned over and gripped her shoulder gently. She looked up into his face.

"Beautiful, Pup," he whispered. "Go on down now."

She nodded and left the loft. A few moments later she was edging in beside Orlando.

There was magic in the cathedral that night, magic in the elusive scent of pine mingled with the pungent frankincense, in the soft glow of the many candles, in the music, and in the rolling phrases of the familiar biblical passages. *In the beginning was the Word, and the Word was with God, and the Word was God* . . . Then came a hymn, and the great cathedral reverberated with the thousands of voices. Alice was awed by the majesty of the sound.

And in the sixth month the angel Gabriel was sent from God, unto a city of Galilee, named Nazareth, to a virgin espoused to a man whose name was Joseph, of the house of David; and the virgin's name was Mary . . . The familiar story unfolded, sounding new and wondrous to Alice. *Then the eyes of the blind shall be opened,* sang the choir, *and the ears of the deaf shall be unstopped: then shall the lame man leap as an hart, and the tongue of the dumb shall sing* . . .

And there were in the same country shepherds abiding in the field . . . Alice, Emery and Christopher slipped quietly up to the organ loft. They stood together by the railing and looked out over the congregation while the rest of the lesson was read. Kenton gave pitches and they began. They sent their voices swirling above the heads of the congregation, eddying and settling like snow. *O wonderful Mystery! O Sacrament divine, passing belief; O wonder! That ox and ass should see the newborn Lord, in slumber lying in the hay.* The last cadence shimmered in the darkness, then settled into silence. The three singers looked at each other; Emery smiled and made a quick, emphatically positive gesture and they hurried back to join the choir.

The service flowed on, easily and swiftly. Though Alice would have liked it to last forever, inexorably it drew to a close. *For ye shall go out with joy, and be led forth with peace: the mountains and the hills shall break forth before you into singing, and all the trees of the field shall clap their hands.*

The organ began the last hymn triumphantly; one by one, the choir members lit their candles and started up the long aisle. As Alice walked and sang, she found herself looking at the people of the congregation, looking for the same sense of mystery, of wonder, on their faces that she felt. She noticed, suddenly, that a man five or six rows away was staring at her intently. When she drew nearer, she stole a glance at him; her mind recoiled in horror — Sir Roderick Donne! She fought back the panic that threatened to overwhelm her, made herself concentrate on the hymn, on her feet. Don't look at him, she told herself. Don't look at anyone. He wouldn't recognize her — he mustn't! And even if he saw a resemblance, he wouldn't be sure. Act normally. Keep singing; keep moving; don't arouse his suspicions.

By the time she reached the back of the nave, she was — outwardly — calm. The choristers formed a group out of the way of the entrance while the hymn finished and the postlude began.

"You were wonderful," Geoffrey told her in a whisper. "I wish you could have seen ol' Frost's face while you sang your solo! *The wolf also shall dwell with the lamb . . .*" He sighed.

Alice smiled. "Thanks. Geoffrey, I want to see Master Kenton. Do you suppose it would be all right if I went up to the organ loft now?"

Geoffrey shrugged. "I don't see why not. Just go up one of the side aisles. I'll wait for you down here."

She nodded and left him. When she reached the loft, she took a seat on one of the benches, closed her eyes, and listened to Kenton's postlude. The music washed over her, calmed her; it was what she needed to give her the courage to go back downstairs and risk coming face to face with the man who had murdered her father.

Kenton finished, changed his shoes, and came over to where she was sitting. He put a hand on her shoulder and looked down at her, a strangely gentle smile on his face.

"Well, Pup," he said softly, "you did us proud."

"It was your piece," she replied. "Don't give me too much credit."

He merely shook his head. "Let's go down. Master Frost probably wants to talk with you."

The crowds had thinned greatly by the time Alice and Kenton went downstairs. She didn't see Sir Roderick, but Master Frost was standing with a group of choir members; they went toward him. When he saw them approaching, a smile lit his face.

"Beautiful, Pup. Just beautiful. Both the solo and

the trio. I was very pleased, and you have every right to be proud of yourself."

"Thank you, sir."

Just then, Dame Agnes came up to them. She was wearing a sprig of holly pinned to her cloak, her only concession to the occasion, but she greeted them effusively.

"Merry Christmas! Master Frost, you've done wonders. The music was lovely." She turned to Alice. "Was that you singing all by yourself? You sounded so angelic. No one listening would guess what a scamp you are! Master Kenton, your playing was delightful — as always." She laid a hand on his arm and smiled coyly at him. "I do hope you'll come to take tea with me again some evening. You're always welcome."

To the delight of Alice and Geoffrey and the utter astonishment of everyone else, Master Kenton replied with perfect civility. "Thank you, ma'am. Perhaps I shall. Merry Christmas."

Alice bit her lips together to hold back her giggles.

"Merry Christmas," Dame Agnes said, then with one last coy smile she went out.

Kenton turned narrowed eyes on Alice and shook a finger at her. "You," he said ominously.

"Do I scent an intrigue brewing?" Emery asked gleefully. "Do tell us, Kenton! Have you lost your heart to that so-charming harpy? 'Dear Master Kenton,' " he mimicked, " 'you're always welcome.' "

Kenton glared at him.

Master Frost, who had watched the exchange with

interest, began to laugh. Master Kenton caught his eye and shook his head ruefully. Then he again looked down at Alice.

"Merry Christmas, Master Kenton," she said with a lurking smile.

He smiled crookedly and ruffled her hair. "Merry Christmas, brat."

"You were absolutely right, Dunstan," Sir Roderick said, grudging respect in his voice. "I'll admit I was skeptical . . ."

"How did she do it?" Lord Crofton wondered aloud. "She ought to have been discovered long ago!"

"Such musings will get you nowhere, gentlemen," Father Cooper chided. "You ought to be applying your minds to the question of what must be done."

"She must disappear," Sir Roderick said with surprising vehemence.

"Now wait a minute. We can't just whisk her out of the choir. There'd be a tremendous hue and cry for her," Lord Crofton protested.

"I beg leave to point out that the choir school is in recess for sixteen days. You ought to be able to make something of that."

"You mean *we* ought to be able to make something of it," Sir Roderick said menacingly. "You're in this, too, Dunstan, you know."

Father Cooper shrugged. "Well, if you can't come up with anything on your own, I have a modest little plan — neat, easy and practically foolproof — but I do think you should at least make an effort to pull your own weight."

"Dunstan," Sir Roderick growled, "I'm getting cursed sick of your attitude."

"Well, I'm getting cursed sick of your bumbling ineptitude," he retorted caustically. "Here's what we'll do — and I devoutly hope you can follow directions." He outlined their plan of action succinctly. "Now, is that clear?"

"Yes. But Dunstan," said Lord Crofton, "what if someone knows she's Alice Tuckfield? That would put a very different face on the matter."

"Don't be absurd. If they knew she was a girl, do you think for a moment they'd let her stay in the choir?"

CHAPTER TWELVE

An enormous jounce woke Alice the next morning. Geoffrey was bouncing on the foot of her bed.

"Wake up, Pup. It's Christmas!"

She blinked at him sleepily. "It was Christmas last night, and you weren't jostling me to death then."

"Yes, but, you silly ninny, there's a Eucharist this morning."

She sat up abruptly. "Good Lord! Then I'd better get up. Merry Christmas, Geoffrey."

"Merry Christmas, Pup." With one final bounce, he got off her bed and went out. Alice rose, slipped into her washing alcove, and dressed quickly; then she ran downstairs and joined the others at breakfast.

The service seemed to drag on and on that morning. All she could think of was the promised party afterward. Twice she was caught daydreaming, and only a sharp nudge from Randall saved her from an embarrassing error. At last it came to an end. She pelted upstairs to the organ loft, hung up her raiment, and raced back downstairs. She was out of the cathedral and running for Dame Agnes's to retrieve the carefully hidden gifts before the postlude was over.

When Alice arrived at the choir room, she stopped short in surprise on the threshold. The room looked completely different. The benches had been pulled back and a large table spread with a white linen cloth had been set up in front of the blazing fire. The table was set with small plates, forks and pewter mugs, and an enormous fruitcake surrounded by holly sat in the center. Alice was recalled to herself by the sound of footsteps behind her. She turned to find Master Hollis, struggling with a steaming punch bowl, coming up the hall. She dodged out of his way.

"Pup!" he exclaimed, after he had set the punch bowl safely down. "Merry Christmas. Is the service over already? I meant to be all ready before you arrived."

"Merry Christmas, Master Hollis," she replied. "Did you make the fruitcake?"

"Bless you, no." He laughed. "We drew lots. I got to mull the cider and set up the room, but Father Cooper has to wash the dishes."

Pup's face fell. "Is he going to be here?"

"Of course. All the masters and all the choir. The Dean usually puts in an appearance as well. But listen: hoofbeats. Here comes the herd."

The rest of the choirboys came thundering into the room, followed more sedately by the choir men and masters. Several people brought plates heaped with things to eat, and in no time the table was full. True to Orlando's prediction, Master Bennett arrived carrying a large tray of cakes with Latin verbs written in icing on their tops. Alice noticed that some of the choir men had brought lutes or viols. When everyone had gathered, Master Frost raised a hand and a hush fell.

"Merry Christmas."

"Merry Christmas," they chorused.

"First of all, I want to thank you all for last night. It was lovely."

There were cheers.

"Furthermore, Lady Genevieve Andrewes, our patroness, sent over some things to help us keep Christmas. The traditional fruitcake," he went on, nodding toward it, "and some new history texts, which Master Hollis said we badly needed. It would be polite of you boys to write her a letter of thanks."

"History texts," Geoffrey whispered in Alice's ear. "*More* books to make us suffer — and Master Frost wants us to *thank* her!"

Master Frost chose to ignore the murmurs. "I think that concludes the business. Why don't you boys line up for your chance at Master Bennett's Latin cakes." He looked over at the master. "The rules are the same, aren't they?"

"With one variation," Master Bennett replied. "I have put pennies in some of the cakes, so some of you will be lucky." He smiled suddenly. "You see, I didn't want any left over this year."

While the choristers lined up for their turn, someone got out a lute and began tuning it. In almost no time, a small group of choir men was taking turns singing lute songs, a fitting accompaniment to the excited, laughing voices of the choristers. At one point when Alice looked around, she saw the Dean standing in the doorway, watching them all. She tried to catch his eye, to wish him Merry Christmas, but before she did Father Cooper had joined him, bringing a mug of the mulled cider and a few comfits and pastries on a plate. Then Father Cooper turned and caught sight of her. The look he gave her was so menacing, it made her tremble. He knows, she thought. Oh, God help me, he *knows!*

"Pup!" The sound of her name made her turn. It was Master Kenton. "Are you all right?"

She tried to smile, but could tell it was a dismal effort. "I must have eaten too many cakes," she said a little shakily. "I don't feel very well."

Master Kenton shook his head. "I'd have said it was Father Cooper who curdled you. I saw that look he gave you. What *have* you been doing to annoy him now?"

"Nothing, I swear it! I don't think he's forgiven me for the Catechism business yet."

Kenton smiled wryly. "I'm sure he hasn't — and won't." He studied her a moment longer. "Don't make yourself sick, Pup. It isn't worth it."

"Hey, Pup, over here!" It was Emery's voice. She

summoned a smile and went over to the little group clustered around the lute. "We need a treble. You must know some of these madrigals."

Alice nodded, and very soon they were all singing.

Across the room, Geoffrey looked up at the sound of Alice's voice. He was beginning to tire of the Latin cakes; he'd found three of the pennies, which was better than most. He felt uneasy about Alice. She had been acting a little strangely, first at the Dean's tea, and right now she didn't look very happy. He noticed Father Cooper and the Dean at the door, and he remembered the strange look the Sub-Dean had given Alice at the Dean's tea. Nodding decisively, he left the line for Master Bennett's cakes and went over to Master Hollis.

"Merry Christmas, Master Hollis."

"Merry Christmas, Geoffrey. Are you having a good time?"

"Yes, sir. Master Hollis, who was it that called Bishop Anscott a senile reprobate in the guise of a cleric?"

Master Hollis's eyebrows shot up. "Now what brought that to your mind?"

"I overheard some people talking about it and I wondered. Do you know?"

"Oh, yes. I don't remember the exact quote, but I know it was Sir Henry Tuckfield. No one else would have dared to insult Bishop Anscott, and it caused quite a stir. The Queen had to intervene in order to keep the bishop from excommunicating him."

Geoffrey frowned thoughtfully.

"Why so pensive?" Master Hollis asked. "It's *Christmas*."

Geoffrey looked up at him and smiled suddenly. "So it is. And we won't have you in class for sixteen whole days!"

Master Hollis smiled. "What a blessed thought."

Geoffrey nodded, then headed for the table. He thought he could squeeze in one more sliver of Mistress Neste's mincemeat pie.

When there was nothing left of the Latin cakes but a few lonely crumbs and the singers had begun on Christmas carols, Alice got out her presents. No one was taking any particular notice of her, so she picked up the catnip and the muffler and went over to where Master Kenton sat. She gave him the catnip first, then put the other package into his hands a little awkwardly.

"That's for Catechism — it's catnip — and this is for you."

Kenton stared at her for a moment, then looked down at the package in his hands. "I don't have anything for you, Pup," he said gruffly.

"But you're teaching me to play," she told him. "That's present enough."

He was motionless a moment longer, then deftly untied the string and shucked the wrapping paper onto the floor. Slowly, he spread out the muffler. He didn't look up at her; she was assailed by doubts. The rich mulberry red looked suddenly too bright, almost garish, to her eyes. The silence stretched on and Alice felt a lump rise in her throat. Finally Kenton spoke, though he still didn't look up.

"It's very nice. Thank you, Pup."

"You're welcome. Merry Christmas, sir." She hoped he couldn't hear the disappointment in her voice. She slipped away, blinking hard. He didn't like it. One fat tear slid down her cheek. She brushed it away hurriedly, hoping no one had seen, and bit her lip resolutely. At least the boys would like her other gift — *if* they liked marzipan. What if they didn't? she thought miserably. But she forced a smile as she picked up the box and gave it to Geoffrey.

"This is really for all of you," she told him, "but you open it, Geoffrey."

He did, and exclamations of wonder and delight came from the other boys. Master Frost smiled.

"How elegant they are," he told her. "They're almost too nice to eat. Where did you find them, Pup?"

"In the marketplace," she replied. "It's a good market — almost as good as a fair."

He nodded. "Well, next time you go there, you'll have this to spend from me." He pressed a penny into her hand. "Merry Christmas."

"Merry Christmas, sir."

Just then, Orlando approached her. "This is for you," he said in a low voice, "from *almost* all of us, but especially from me, Nate, Geoffrey, Timothy and Randall." He put a package into her hands.

She unwrapped it quickly: a pair of dark green woolen mittens.

"To keep those keyboard hands of yours warm," he added.

"Thank you. They're wonderful." She put them on and clapped experimentally. "Now I'll really be able to pack snowballs!"

A little while later the party broke up. It had started to snow again, and Alice lagged a little behind the others; their talk was all of going home, and somehow she didn't want to hear it. She was frightened and worried and disappointed. She wasn't feeling at all festive; in fact, she didn't really see how things could get much worse. She was reasonably certain that Father Cooper knew who she was, but she was afraid to take Master Hunnis's advice and go to the Dean. Father Cooper seemed so friendly with him — what if he was in on the plot, too? She wished she dared confide in someone. She had thought of telling Geoffrey, but while she knew he would probably believe her, she really didn't see how he could help. She had considered explaining her situation to Master Kenton, but she was very much afraid he wouldn't believe her. And then, she thought glumly, I really *would* be in the stew.

Master Kenton . . . Even the thought of him was depressing. He didn't like the muffler; it had probably been a terrible mistake to give it to him at all. It had probably embarrassed him dreadfully — and she had only meant to please him.

With an effort, she wrenched her thoughts away from him. She needed to consider what to do about Father Cooper. Perhaps she should run away to Master Hunnis in London. At least he knew who she was and would be willing to help her. Of course, London was a long way and she had almost no money, thanks to the muffler.

"What a *fool* I am," she muttered angrily.

There *was* Lady Jenny — *if* she were back from France and *if* Father Cooper were no longer watching Chellisford Hall. Too many ifs. They circled in her brain like bats at dusk. If Father Cooper knew who she was, he was bound to act soon, especially if he suspected that she knew that he knew. But *what*, she wondered, would he *do?*

She was so lost in her own thoughts that she didn't see the large man emerge from an alleyway, and she walked straight into him. She was knocked off balance but was somehow held upright by the folds of the heavy cloth of his cloak. She got her feet under her and tried to pull away, but she was held fast. She began to struggle. Then she heard Master Kenton's voice call her name behind her, and an instant later she pulled free of the cloak. Father Cooper was frowning at her sternly. She gasped.

"You should watch where you're going, young fellow. You might have been hurt."

"I — I'm sorry, Father," she managed to say.

"Merry Christmas, Father Cooper," Kenton called as he came up to them. Alice looked at him with relief.

"Merry Christmas, Master Kenton," Father Cooper said stiffly, then turned on his heel and went away down the street.

"Pup," Kenton began tentatively, then his gaze sharpened. "Pup, what on earth is the matter? You're trembling!"

"I'm cold," she said hurriedly.

He scowled in irritation. "It's Father Cooper, isn't it? Why are you so afraid of him, Pup?"

"I'm not afraid," she said emphatically. "I'm cold."

He studied her for a moment, then shrugged. "Well, let's not argue about it. Pup, what I really want to talk to you about is —" He sighed, clearly ill at ease. "I don't think I thanked you properly at the party."

She took a deep breath. Then she noticed he was wearing the muffler; surely he was just being kind.

"I was rather . . ." He paused, searching for a word.

"Aghast?" she supplied a little sharply. Then she bit her lip and studied her feet.

He took her by the shoulders and gave her a gentle shake. "Look at me!"

Reluctantly, she raised her eyes to his face.

"Pup, none of my students has ever given me a Christmas present before. I was surprised and — touched." He hunched one shoulder ruefully. "I didn't know what to say. But I really do like it."

She studied his face in silence. "It's not too bright?" she asked at last.

He ruffled her hair. "It's beautiful, Pup. Come on. I'll walk you home."

"But the Dame will make you take tea with her," she said mischievously.

He looked down at her, smiling a little crookedly. "I won't come in. I'll leave you at the door."

Alice shook her head. "She'll be disappointed."

"She'll never know if you don't *tell* her," he pointed out.

Soon Kenton left her at the kitchen door. "Merry Christmas, Pup."

"Merry Christmas." She turned and bounded up the stairs, grinning. He *does* like it, she said to herself with satisfaction. She felt better. There was probably even a solution to her other problems. Maybe she would speak to Geoffrey after all, but she wouldn't worry anymore, at least not today. Today was *Christmas*.

CHAPTER THIRTEEN

Alice decided to speak to Geoffrey that afternoon, before he left for his grandmother's. She knew he would be gone by suppertime, and she thought she might sleep better if someone else knew about her troubles. Besides, she was pretty sure he suspected something was wrong, and she wanted to tell him before he asked her about it. She found him in their sleeping quarters, packing up some things he wanted to take with him.

"Hi, Pup," he said when he saw her.

She came over and sat down on the foot of his bed, wrapping herself up in one of the spare blankets lying there. It was cold in the room. "Geoffrey, I need to talk to you."

"All right, but can't we go downstairs? It's warmer in the kitchen."

"No. I'm sorry, but I want to talk to you alone."

He nodded, then sat down on the bed and picked up

the other spare blanket. For a long moment Alice was silent, looking down at her hands as she picked lint off the woolen blanket. At last she sighed.

"I didn't think this would be so hard. Geoffrey, I'm in trouble — in danger, I believe. You see, my father was murdered and —" Her voice caught, and she went on in a whisper. "— and I witnessed it. I know the men who killed him and I can identify them, and they either know or suspect that." She took a deep breath and went on in a more normal tone. "Did you ever wonder about those men in the cathedral that night?"

Geoffrey nodded, his eyes wide.

"They were my father's murderers. They were there to meet the other conspirator, the one who planned it: Father Cooper."

"Father *Cooper!*" Geoffrey exclaimed, his eyes opening wide in alarm. "But Pup! I think he knows who you are! He heard you talking about your father and what he said to Bishop Anscott."

She nodded. "I know. I saw his face." Her calm façade shattered. "Geoffrey, I'm so frightened!"

Awkwardly, he put a hand on her shoulder. "Now Pup," he said, trying to sound bracing, "don't worry. We'll think of something."

"But they — they're going to k-kill me," she said, fighting back tears.

"Not if I can help it," he said staunchly. "Now, what can we do? We could go to Master Frost," he suggested.

"What if he didn't believe me?"

"He'd have to. After all, it's true."

Alice made a face. "You're such a pair of scamps," she mimicked. "Next time, try a slightly less fantastic tale. Now run along and don't bother me."

"But even then, Pup, what have we lost? And he might believe us — you can't be sure."

She shook her head.

"Well, we could go to the magistrate."

Her eyes widened suddenly in alarm. "Oh, good Lord! No we *can't*. I forgot to tell you: the murderers were acting on the Queen's orders — at least they said that Her Majesty would be pleased."

Geoffrey frowned in concentration. "Wait a minute, Pup," he said at last. "If they acted with the Queen's approval, why would they bother to kill you? Would it really matter if you could identify them if the Queen were going to shield them? It doesn't make sense."

"I don't know, Geoffrey, but I don't want to take the chance. We'll have to think of something else."

He nodded. "What about your old master — the one who visited you? Does he know who you are?"

She nodded.

"And he didn't tell Master Kenton or Master Frost?" Geoffrey asked incredulously. "That's amazing!"

"I made him promise not to. Geoffrey, if I went to London, I know he'd help me, but how on earth would I get there? I haven't any money to speak of, and I couldn't *possibly* walk."

"Then that's not the answer. It's a pity he isn't closer to home."

She nodded. "There's an old friend of my father's

who lives at Chellisford Hall. Do you know where that is?"

"Yes. It's about eight miles outside of the city walls, on the road to Leeds. So why not go there?"

"Well, I would, except that when I first came to the cathedral, I overheard Father Cooper say that Lady Jenny was in France and that he would watch Chellisford Hall. What if he's still watching or Lady Jenny is still in France?"

Geoffrey raised his eyebrows. "It's the dead of winter, Pup. How likely is he to be spending all his time shivering in the snow? We all know how much he values his comfort."

"Yes, but it needn't be *him* watching. There are the other two, as well."

"That's a point," he conceded, "but —"

Just then, Dame Agnes's voice called upstairs. "Geoffrey! Your grandmother is here!"

"Coming!" he replied. "Oh, Lord," he added to Alice. "Now listen here: I'll come back tomorrow — or as soon as I can get away — and we'll figure out what to do. In the meantime, don't go *anywhere* alone, and don't tell any of the others what you've told me — there's always the chance that the wrong ears will hear of it. Remember, *don't go out alone*. Stay inside if you can."

Alice smiled wryly. "The Dame is going to love me."

He shrugged. "At least it will give you plenty of practice at making up excuses! It shouldn't be too bad — a day or two at the most. And you *do* see my point, don't you?"

She nodded.

"*Geoffrey!*" They heard irritation in the Dame's voice and, a moment later, her footsteps on the stairs.

"Coming!" he cried, grabbing his satchel and dashing out the door. Alice watched him go; with a sigh, she folded the blankets and went back down to the relative warmth of the kitchen.

The day after Christmas it turned bitterly cold. The snow groaned underfoot and noses and ears grew nearly numb just in the short trip from the kitchen to the woodshed and back. Alice, Orlando and the three other boys who had stayed at the school spent most of their time huddled near the kichen fire. Alice realized that Geoffrey wouldn't be able to come until it got warmer, and, though inwardly she chafed at the delay, she managed to preserve an outward calm. At least, she thought, the Dame could hardly fault her for remaining inside. There was little to do in the house (especially since one had to stay near a fire in order to stay warm), so Alice and Orlando passed the time tutoring each other, to the disgust of the others.

"Latin and Theory," Alice groaned late in the afternoon of the third day of the cold spell. "Some vacation."

Orlando nodded gloomily and edged closer to the fire. "If it ever warms up, we can go skating. The Foss is bound to be frozen after all this."

"I don't have any skates." She sighed. "I wonder what's for supper."

The Dame looked around from the counter where she was working. "Blood pudding," she said tartly. "And you can take that look off your face! There are plenty of little boys who'd be happy to have a nice blood pudding for supper."

"They can have mine," Alice muttered to Orlando — but not softly enough.

The Dame stomped across the room, brandishing a wooden spoon. "Now, you listen here!" she snapped. "You've been surly and disagreeable all day long, and I'm tired of it. You've been acting as though someone planned this weather solely to annoy *you*. Do you think I enjoy having all of you underfoot the whole day? This cold is hard on us all — not just you. Now, do your Latin and stop complaining!" Dame Agnes went back to her work. Alice watched her with resentful eyes.

"*I'm* surly and disagreeable?" she grumbled. "What does that make *her?*"

Orlando shook his head warningly, but it was too late. The Dame charged across the room, grabbed Alice's ear, and hauled her to her feet. "I've had enough of your impertinence, Pup! You're going to bed now, with no supper, and I don't want to hear a single squeak out of you. Now, go!" She rapped Alice smartly across the back with the wooden spoon and shoved her toward the door. Alice stalked off, her chin high and her lips pressed firmly together. She was furiously angry.

"And you should count your blessings, young man, that you didn't get a beating, for you richly deserve one!" the Dame called after her.

A couple of hours later, Orlando tiptoed to the side of Alice's bed. "Pup?" he whispered. "I brought you some bread from dinner."

"Thanks."

"You've got to be wary of the Dame when she's like this — foul-tempered as a caged bear. Maybe it will be warmer tomorrow."

"I'll never be warm again," Alice said glumly.

"I have to go back down," he said. "But I tell you what. I'll try to heat a brick for you when she isn't looking." He started away.

"Don't get caught, for heaven's sake," she whispered after him, but he just smiled.

The next morning it *was* warmer. The wind had brought clouds, heavy with snow, and though the day was dark and the sky threatening, they all greeted the change with enthusiasm. As they got out their sleds and skates, Alice watched with misgiving.

"What's the matter, Pup?" Orlando asked as he began wrapping his muffler around his neck. "Aren't you coming with us?"

"No thanks, Orlando. I think I'd rather stay here."

"Well, you can just think again, Alister Tucker," the Dame said rather sharply. "You're not going to mope around here under my feet all day."

"I don't feel very well," Alice protested. "I really don't want to spend the day outside."'

"Nonsense! The fresh air will do you *worlds* of good," the Dame insisted. "Now get your outdoor things."

"But —"

"No more arguing. The matter is closed."

Alice looked at the Dame's stern face and crossed arms and realized further protests would be futile. "Wait for me, Orlando," she said.

He nodded, and shortly the little group was on its way to the Foss.

There was a holiday atmosphere about the river. People had built fires along the banks, some even on the ice, and a few enterprising vendors had set up stalls and were doing a brisk trade in hot meat pies and other delicacies. Alice bought two sticky sweet rolls, one for herself and one for Orlando, and they sat on a wharf eating them and watching some skaters.

"Pup! Orlando!"

They turned at the sound of their names.

"Geoffrey!" they cried together.

With a grin, he joined them. "The Dame told me you were here — I stopped in on my way. You aren't going to sit here all day, are you? Randall's here, and he brought his sled."

"Where?" Orlando asked eagerly.

"Over there. Look!" He pointed to a group of children clustered around a sled. "Come on and we'll give you a ride."

As they watched, several of the bigger boys took the

sled rope and began to run, pulling a laughing load of the others along the ice.

"Come on, Pup, let's go," Orlando said, getting to his feet.

She looked a little doubtful, but rose also. Orlando set off toward the others, not waiting to see whether she was coming. Geoffrey looked at her with concern.

"Look, Pup," he said quietly as they started after Orlando, "there really isn't much Father Cooper and his friends can do in a huge crowd of people — especially if you stay near one of us all the time."

"I suppose not," she said with a sigh. "I just don't feel very cheerful."

He nodded. "Well, at least you can pretend to be. Come on, let's hurry."

The day passed quickly. Nate joined them a little after noon, and they all went on an exploratory expedition upriver, but their adventure was curtailed when they began to get cold. They turned back to the bustling center of town and found a fire to get warm beside. Someone started a snowball fight and then a game of snatch-the-hat, and almost before they knew it it had begun to get dark.

"It's gotten late all of a sudden," Nate said. "I must get home. If you're all going back into town, I'll go with you."

The others nodded and they set off. Geoffrey dropped back to speak with Alice.

"I'm off home. Gram doesn't live too far from here."

He shook a reproving finger at Alice's alarmed expression. "Now Pup," he chided, "you know very well that Orlando's going back to the Dame's with you, so there's nothing to worry about. Tomorrow perhaps we can go to Chellisford Hall — I have a friend with a sledge. Don't worry so, and I'll see you in the morning." Then he pitched his voice so all of them could hear. "I'm off home. I'll see you tomorrow."

"Goodnight, Geoffrey," the others replied, waving as he went down the street.

The others watched him go, then started back themselves. When they reached the Star Inn, Nate said good-bye and turned off the main street toward his home.

"See you tomorrow," he called over his shoulder.

As they neared the Minster close, they heard the hour strike. Randall stopped short in dismay. "Good Lord! I had no idea it was so late. We must run, or Mam will skin us. Pup, would you mind telling the Dame where Orlando is? I've asked him over to dinner and to spend the night. I'd have invited you, too, but Mam said one at a time."

Alice stared at them in horror. "You aren't going to walk me home?"

Randall laughed. "You know the way, and we're late already. Be a sport, Pup, and we'll see you tomorrow."

"But —" she began desperately.

"Cut through the Bedern and the Minster close," Orlando advised. "It's faster. Thanks again — and see you tomorrow."

"Orlando, *wait*," she called after him as he and Randall started off at a trot.

"There's no time," he replied over his shoulder. Then they were gone.

Alice took a deep breath and bit her lips together. It wasn't far, she told herself. It really wasn't far, and she had seen no sign of Father Cooper or any of them all day. She'd just have to trust to luck.

The storm that had held off all day chose that moment to break. It caught her off guard. The wind came howling down Goodramgate with the snow at its heels. Alice decided she'd better cut through the Bedern and Minster close after all; it was hard for her to distinguish any landmarks with the snow, and she knew she could find her way home from the cathedral *asleep* if need be. Besides, she told herself, unless Father Cooper had been following her all day, he wouldn't see her in all this snow unless she tripped over him. Resolutely, she turned up Vicar Lane.

From the shadow of a doorway, Father Cooper watched her. He might never have taken any notice of the children if he hadn't heard their voices. Orlando was not a common name, and Alice knew how to make herself heard. With a small, smug smile, he started up Vicar Lane after her.

The Minster close was deserted, a strange wasteland of wind and snow. As Alice struck across toward the Minster gates, moving like a shadow, she didn't see the cloaked figure following stealthily. As she passed the south door of the Minster, Father Cooper made his move. Taking several rapid steps, he caught up with Alice and grabbed her. She opened her mouth to scream, but a fleshy hand stifled the sound. She squirmed frantically but couldn't free herself, so she bit the hand as hard as she could.

"You cursed little imp of Satan!" Father Cooper hissed, cuffing her roughly with his other hand.

Alice tasted blood in her mouth and struggled fiercely. She loosened her grip, and suddenly the hand was pulled away. She filled her lungs to scream, but Father Cooper's hands closed around her throat tightly enough to make the world spin sickly.

"One sound," he ground out, "and I'll kill you."

She ceased her struggles abruptly, watching him with wide, frightened eyes. That he hadn't already killed her surprised her; perhaps he didn't mean to kill her right away. As she ceased her struggles, his hold relaxed very slightly. Carefully, fearfully, she worked one of her mittens loose and let it fall to the ground. They were near the cathedral; it was possible — barely — that it might act as a clue. Then Alice heard footsteps. This might be her chance! She kicked Father Cooper in the shin with every ounce of strength she possessed. He winced and cursed under his breath; his hands tightened further, and Alice's world dissolved into spinning darkness.

Master Kenton came out of the cathedral and pulled the heavy south door shut behind him. He scowled at the snow and wound his new muffler more snugly around his neck. With a sigh, he went down the steps and started toward the Bedern. As he scuffed along through the snow, he kicked a mitten lying on the ground, a small, green mitten, just big enough for —

"Pup," he said aloud. He bent and picked it up. Careless of the boy, he thought. He smiled faintly and put the mitten in his pocket, imagining how relieved Pup would be to get it back.

CHAPTER FOURTEEN

Alice opened her eyes, then blinked. Her first thought was that she'd been struck blind. Her mind felt fuzzy and her head ached. She tried to reach up and rub a hand over her eyes, but, strangely, her hands wouldn't obey her. Slowly, her mind cleared. She was lying on her side; her wrists were tied behind her and her ankles bound together; a wad of cloth was stuffed in her mouth, held in place by another, tied tightly enough to choke her. She was cold and stiff and her throat felt bruised and swollen.

Despair washed over her. Where was she? What would they do to her? For a moment, she wondered why Father Cooper hadn't killed her. The old hypocrite had probably hired someone else to do the deed, she thought, then shuddered. She could still feel his horrid hands around her throat. At least I bit him, she thought. I hope he dies of it.

Gradually, she became aware of strange noises: a

faint creaking sound, then a groan, then a thump, quite loud, behind her. She wanted to squirm about to look, but she closed her eyes and made herself lie still. It had sounded like a trap door opening.

". . . don't understand why you didn't finish the job. It would have spared us this effort." That sounded like Lord Crofton. Alice suppressed a shudder.

"Because, you fool, we need to know what she knows!" That was Father Cooper. There was a grunt and a thump, then footsteps. "She's still out. What's keeping Roderick?"

"Nothing," Sir Roderick Donne snapped. "Damned ladder."

"She knows too much, Dunstan, any way you cut it," Lord Crofton pointed out. "See if you can't bring her round. I'd like to get this over with."

A moment later Alice saw a faint light through her eyelids. A foot nudged her, and, to her utter surprise, water was dashed in her face. She stifled a gasp and moaned faintly. Then she let her eyelids flutter open.

"Now, pay attention," Father Cooper instructed. "In a moment I am going to remove the gag. However, no outcry you may think of making will do any good at all. I want you to answer some questions, but my friends think it a waste of time. They would be delighted to kill you without further ado, and if you try anything at all I shall let them. Is that clear?"

Alice managed to nod; the priest bent down and undid the gag. She noticed with satisfaction that his right hand was bandaged.

"Now, do you know who murdered your father?"

"Yes," Alice croaked. It hurt terribly to speak, but she forced the words out. She was gambling, but she knew it was her only chance. "You planned it, and Sir Roderick Donne and Lord Crofton did the deed, and it won't do you any good to kill me because I told someone it was you."

"Good God!" Sir Roderick exclaimed.

"It's a bluff," Father Cooper said calmly. "And even if it isn't, what does it matter if she told one of her choirboy friends. No one is going to take a child's word against ours."

"If that's true, why kill me at all?" she asked.

"Dunstan, I —"

While the three men argued, Alice did some rapid figuring in her head. It was a long shot, but she'd have to chance it. It was imperative that they believe her, or at least believe the threat real enough to bear looking into. She must buy time. Then, perhaps, a chance of escape would present itself.

"Whom did you tell?" Sir Roderick Donne stood looking down at her threateningly.

She met his gaze squarely. "I told Master William Hunnis," she answered, watching him intently. The force of his reaction startled her. His face went ashen.

"Christ! Crofton, we're doomed. He's such a favorite now, he'll be bound to tell the Queen."

"Hold your tongue, fool," Crofton barked. "This can't be true. How could she tell him? Write a letter?"

Father Cooper frowned. "Hunnis was in York before

Christmas. Apparently Kenton had written him about young 'Alister Tucker.' She had the chance, Crofton, but whether or not she did, I can't say. He must have known who she is, but why didn't he tell Frost? Or the Dean, if he were worried about her safety?" He shook his head.

Sir Roderick approached Alice menacingly. "I'll find out what she told him," he growled.

Father Cooper intercepted him. "Yes, you will. One of you will have to make discreet inquiries at Court —"

"Do you think I'm stupid enough to walk into a trap like that? Let me warn you, Dunstan: if I fall, I'm pulling you down with me!"

"Who said anything about falling, fool?" Father Cooper snapped. "What have you got inside that skull? Oak? If — and I repeat, if — you should find yourself in, er, a difficult situation, use the child's life for a bargaining piece. If the Queen is too fastidious to be grateful when a truly prime nuisance like Henry Tuckfield is neatly disposed of, she'll be much too squeamish to want the girl's blood on her hands. Or, given her fondness for musicians, you could tell her young Alice is a very talented little singer — it's true enough. With a little finesse, you ought to be able to get free pardons out of it — or at the least banishments."

"And if she's bluffing?"

"Oh, for heaven's sake, do you need everything spelled out for you? We do away with her and dump her body in the North Sea!"

Alice swallowed painfully and forced herself to think

173

about the time she had bought — possibly as much as a week.

"Except for this minor revision," Father Cooper went on, "we'll stick to the plan. Roderick, you can take care of the letter on your way out of town. We'll draft it tonight." He bent down and picked up the gag.

"I'm hungry," Alice whispered hoarsely.

"Damn," he replied. He unceremoniously stuffed the gag back into her mouth. "I'll be back."

Alice saw the lantern light retreat, watched the curious jumble of shadows on the wall as the men left; she heard the same faint creaking noise as before but no thump; then the footsteps faded away and she was left in silence and darkness.

How long she waited she didn't know, but it was long enough for her to become painfully aware of the stiffness of her arms and legs and of the cold. Finally, she heard noises again and saw Father Cooper and his lantern. He came over to her, knelt down, and removed the gag, then pulled her roughly into a sitting position and began spooning gruel into her. Her throat was so sore it hurt to swallow, and the gruel had a strange, bitter aftertaste, but she made herself eat, realizing there was no knowing when he'd feed her again. When he finished, he reached again for the gag.

"Please," she whispered hoarsely. "Please don't gag me again. I'll be quiet."

He picked up the gag and stuffed it back into her mouth. "Come, come," he chided. "I'm not fool enough to expect you to keep such a promise. I'd think you an idiot if you did with your life at stake." He gave her a rough shove and knocked her back onto her side and tossed a blanket over her; then he picked up the lantern and went to the trap door. She heard creaking sounds and the light grew fainter, but again there was no thump of the door. A moment later Father Cooper returned, carrying a brazier and a large sack of wood. Deftly, he laid a fire and lit it, sitting back on his heels to watch the smoke as it rose to the high ceiling and filtered out through the chinks. Then he rose and went back to the trap door. She heard it groan, then thump shut, and she was again alone. Somewhere, quite near at hand, a bell tolled eight times. She puzzled over it for a moment, but her mind was going fuzzy again; darkness swooped in, in great swirling clouds. Two thoughts lurked, barely out of reach, and she stretched for them; but before she could catch hold of them, unconsciousness again washed over her.

The Dame was annoyed when Orlando and Pup were late for supper. The other boys had told her they'd been with Randall, Geoffrey and Nate, so she wasn't alarmed. The wretched boys had probably gone home to eat with one of the other boys and had neglected to send her word. But as the hours slipped by and there was still no word of her missing charges, she began to feel uneasy.

"They probably decided to stay the night," she said, "what with the snow. Those naughty, inconsiderate lads — they should have seen to it that I knew." But her uneasiness grew; it wasn't like Orlando or Pup simply to leave her to worry. When the clock on the mantel struck eleven, she decided to go to bed. Time enough to worry about the boys in the morning, when something could be done.

Father Cooper's pen scratched along as Lord Crofton paced before the fire and Sir Roderick sat fidgeting with his wineglass.

"There," said the priest at last, dusting the sheet with fine sand and shaking it off. While he rummaged about for the sealing wax, Sir Roderick and Lord Crofton came over to the desk and read the letter.

"Just the right tone," Lord Crofton said approvingly. "Sentimental enough but not quite maudlin. And the little hints and innuendoes — marvelous. No one would dream of interfering. Long-lost nephew and prosperous, childless merchant uncle reunited. Dunstan, you're brilliant."

The priest preened a little. "That should keep the old harpy quiet until Epiphany — plenty of time. Now, Roderick, remember the plan. As soon as the cursed snow lets up, find an urchin to deliver this to Dame Agnes Mauperley, at Number Four Fletcher Street."

"What if the urchin recognizes me?"

"Oh, for God's sake, Roddy," Father Cooper snapped, exasperated. "Just pull your hood up around your face and there won't be any problems."

"You're very glib," he complained, "but it's not as if it were your neck."

"Oh, but it is, Roderick," he said with surprising grimness. "Oh, but it is."

The morning dawned clear and inviting. The wind had sculpted the new snow into an unfamiliar land-scape of dunes and drifts. Geoffrey could hardly wait to get out in it. He gobbled down his porridge with more haste than appreciation and asked his grand-mother if he could be excused. She assented, and in a scant few minutes he was slamming the door behind himself. He floundered cheerfully off through the snow toward the Dame's.

When he reached the Mermaid Inn he slowed his pace, as much to watch the activity in the innyard as to catch his breath. The Mermaid was a handsome, half-timbered structure with diamond-paned leaded win-dows; a sign painted with its namesake hung over the door. The cobbled yard was large and, miraculously, swept clean of snow. One of the ostlers was bringing a neat bay hack around from the stables while several people bustled about near the doorway.

Geoffrey watched for a moment, then turned and started off. But before he had gone more than a few steps, a voice brought him up short.

"Boy!"

He turned to find a man, heavily muffled against the cold, approaching him.

"Sir?" Geoffrey inquired, sketching a bow.

"Would you like to earn a ha'penny?"

"Yes, sir," Geoffrey replied enthusiastically. But at

the back of his mind, he had a nagging sense that this man was familiar to him, a sense he could neither shake nor place.

The man pulled a sealed letter out of the folds of his cloak and handed it to the boy. "Take this to the lady who lives at Number Four Fletcher Street."

"Sh-shall I wait for an answer?" he asked, hoping his surprise wasn't too apparent. A letter for Dame Agnes from a gentleman?

"No, no. That won't be necessary." He flipped a halfpence to Geoffrey, who caught it neatly. "Hurry now, boy."

Geoffrey started off briskly, looking back just in time to see the man swing easily up into the saddle and start out of the innyard. Geoffrey was still puzzling over what made the man seem so familiar. It couldn't be his face; Geoffrey hadn't gotten a good look at it, between the hood and the muffler. Suddenly, he stopped short. "People don't just disappear": he heard the words clearly in his mind, spoken in the voice of the man who had just given him the letter. That was it! The voice. It reminded him of the voice of the stranger in the cathedral. "It just reminds me of it," he told himself firmly. It was too ridiculous, too wildly improbable; he was getting as jumpy as Pup. With an effort, he dismissed it from his mind.

When he reached the Dame's, he found the breakfast cleanup in full swing, with Dame Agnes herself supervising. She rounded on Geoffrey almost before he had closed the door.

"Where's Pup?" she demanded.

Geoffrey's heart skipped a beat, but he forced himself to reply with his usual blitheness. "How on earth would I know? Dodged out on the cleanup, has he?" He handed the letter to her. "A gentleman gave this to me to give to you."

She hardly glanced at it. "Pup wasn't with you last night? Or Orlando?"

He shook his head. "Do you mean that neither Pup nor Orlando came home?"

"Yes." The Dame pushed at a wisp of hair distractedly. "Could they be with Nate or Randall, do you suppose?"

"Oh dear God," he whispered; then he realized the Dame was waiting for an answer. "I didn't hear them mention anything of the kind. I thought they were both going straight home."

Just then, the door burst open again and Orlando and Randall came in.

"Oh, good. We caught you," Orlando said cheerfully. "I don't suppose there's any tea hot. It's colder than yesterday's porridge out there!"

"Orlando, where have you been?" the Dame demanded. "And where is Pup?"

"I was with Randall. Didn't Pup tell you? He said he would."

"Pup didn't come home last night," she said heavily.

"What?" Randall demanded. "But he *couldn't* have gotten lost. We left him near Goodramgate. He was going to cut through the Bedern and the close."

Geoffrey sat down abruptly on the bench, his face white. "Pup went through the Minster close last night *alone?*" he whispered, horrified. "Oh, dear God." Then, as he noticed the others' curious stares, he recovered himself abruptly. "Dame Agnes, what does the letter say?"

"Letter? Geoffrey, how can you —" She stopped, looking down at the letter in her hands. With a brisk movement she broke the seal, unfolded the heavy sheet, and began to read. Slowly the anxious look on her face was replaced by relief.

"It's from Pup's uncle," she told the boys. "Pup's with him. He's been looking for Pup for months, now. He was on his way to visit me when he ran into Pup. He was so surprised and delighted that he took Pup off to have dinner with him — completely forgetting his duty to let me know! But he's so contrite and so obviously happy to have found his nephew" — Geoffrey's head came up and he met Orlando's eye — "that I'm inclined to forgive him."

"Where's Pup now?" Geoffrey demanded.

"Master Tucker has taken him to his home in Knaresborough to spend the rest of the holiday. Pup's a lucky boy," she added, a slightly calculating gleam coming into her eyes. "It sounds as though his uncle is quite well off." She looked around the room a little severely. "Hurry up and finish in here, boys," she advised, then left the kitchen.

"I'll bet anything Pup's uncle isn't married," Randall said in an undertone. "That's the only reason she could have turned sweet so fast. Maybe next time you're in trouble, Geoffrey, you can invent a rich, unattached uncle to get you out of it."

Geoffrey's face was pale and worried. "It's a lie. I know it is."

"Oh, Geoffrey." Randall sighed. "Can't you just be happy for Pup's good fortune without turning it into a grand drama?"

Noting the curiosity of the other choristers, Geoffrey bit back a hot retort and gestured toward the door. "Let's go out where we can talk."

Randall rolled his eyes but followed when Orlando led the way to the door. Once outside, they had to keep moving to stay warm, so they wandered through the maze of alleys near the cathedral.

"Now, Geoffrey, perhaps you can explain why you don't believe in Pup's uncle," Randall suggested.

"Well, for one thing, he talks about his *nephew*," Geoffrey began.

"What do you expect?" Randall retorted, exasperated. "The Dame doesn't know the truth about Pup. I bet Pup made him say 'nephew' so we wouldn't get into trouble."

"I didn't think of that," Orlando put in.

"But Tucker isn't Pup's real name," Geoffrey protested.

"Maybe it's Pup's mother's maiden name."

"I know you think I'm mad, Randall, but I'm not! There are just too many coincidences." In a tight, strained voice, Geoffrey repeated what Alice had told him about her father's murder and Father Cooper's involvement. The others listened in stunned silence.

"Pup should have *told* us!" Orlando cried when Geoffrey had finished. "We'd have walked her home if we'd known."

Randall shook his head remorsefully. "I knew *something* was bothering Pup, but I wouldn't stay to find out what. But done is done, I fear. The question is, what should we do now?"

"I think we should go to Master Kenton," Geoffrey said with resolution.

"Sourface?" Orlando blurted. "You're out of your mind!"

"No, I'm not! He likes Pup. Besides, he's a friend of that old master of Pup's — the one who came to visit. Maybe he knows something."

"You're planning to tell him all about Pup, aren't you?" Randall asked.

Geoffrey nodded seriously. "If Pup has been kidnapped, we are the only chance she has. I don't think we have any choice but to tell someone, and Kenton *will* help — if we can make him believe us. I'm going. Are you with me?"

The others nodded. Randall studied Geoffrey's face for a long moment. "Geoffrey," he said quietly, "I'm sorry. I should have listened to you when you first brought all this up. I hope —" His voice caught. "I mean, Geoffrey," he said very gently, "if what you suspect is true, they — it may already be too late."

Geoffrey's brow knit. "I know. But if they were

just going to kill her, why bother with the letter at all? They must be trying to buy time for some reason." Then his calm demeanor crumbled, and his voice shook as he whispered, "It's the only hope we have."

The three boys turned and set off briskly, Geoffrey leading the way.

CHAPTER FIFTEEN

Master Kenton was not in the cathedral when Geoffrey, Orlando and Randall got there, but the old verger was puttering about.

"Sir." Geoffrey went up to him boldly. "Do you know where Master Kenton is?"

The verger regarded them dubiously. "You've missed him. He was here for Matins. I expect he's gone home to his breakfast."

"Where does he live?" Geoffrey persisted. "It's urgent we see him."

"Urgent mischief, I daresay," the verger retorted tartly. "I know your rascally ways."

"I swear it isn't!" Geoffrey said. "On a stack of Bibles, if you like."

"Oh, yes," the old man said, unimpressed. "And you'd swear if it was, just the same."

"Randall wouldn't. Ask him!"

The verger turned to Randall. "It's true, you aren't such a scamp as the others. Is it true? You aren't up to mischief?"

"We aren't up to anything, and it is frightfully important that we see Master Kenton."

The verger sighed. "Well, he'll probably have my head for telling you — a nasty temper the man has, and no mistake — but if you say it's important . . ." He hesitated. "He lives in Alewife Lane, next to the Mermaid Inn. Number Six, I think it is. You know where that is?"

"Yes," Geoffrey said. "Thank you, sir," he added as they tore off.

A few minutes later they were pounding on Master Kenton's door. "Coming, coming." His voice came impatiently from within. "I'm not all that deaf." The door swung open, and he stared at the boys. "You! I thought I was free of you until after Epiphany. What do you want?"

"Pup's missing, sir," Geoffrey blurted out. "He didn't go home last night."

"*Missing?*" Master Kenton repeated. Then he opened the door wider. "Well, come on in. There's no sense in freezing on the doorstep. Sit down." He motioned them to chairs by a blazing fire. Catechism was sprawled on the hearth rug, sound asleep. The boys seated themselves while Master Kenton took his place standing by the fire. He regarded them impassively for a moment while they shifted uncomfortably. Then he said, with a touch of impatience, "Well?"

"I don't really know how to start," Geoffrey confessed.

"Try the beginning," Master Kenton suggested dryly.

"Well, sir, the truth is that Pup's real name isn't Alister Tucker at all," Geoffrey began. Noticing the master's skepticism, he hurried on. "It's really Alice Tuckfield, and we think she's been kidnapped."

"*Alice?* Good God, do you mean Pup's a girl?"

Geoffrey nodded.

"Geoffrey, if this is a prank, I swear to God I'll —"

"It's not!" he protested. "We met Pup on the street. I ran into her and knocked her down, and she looked hungry, so we took her home and gave her supper. And then we found out she could sing, and we thought it would be a grand lark to see how long she could hide in the choir without old Frost noticing, and then he let Pup in officially — and now she's been kidnapped."

"How do you know Pup's been kidnapped? Maybe he — I mean she — is with Nate."

"Wouldn't that be just our luck," Orlando muttered pessimistically.

"But the letter, Orlando!" Geoffrey argued.

"What letter?" Kenton asked.

"There was a letter that a man at the Mermaid gave me to give to Dame Agnes. It was supposedly from Pup's uncle — a 'Master Tucker' (which isn't even her real name) who was taking her off to Knaresborough for the holiday. But —"

"Geoffrey Fisher, are you *certain* this isn't a prank?"

"Yes!"

"Then you had better explain what's wrong with Pup having an uncle. I swear I've never heard such a farfetched load of nonsense!"

Geoffrey eyed him seriously for a moment. "Master, do you remember the night you found Pup and me in the cathedral?"

Master Kenton's eyes narrowed and he nodded.

"Do you remember how *spooked* Pup was?"

Again, Kenton nodded.

"Well, Pup knew more about those men than she let on. That's why she was so scared. Those men were the ones who murdered Sir Henry, and Pup —"

"Sir Henry?" Kenton interrupted, then his eyes widened. "Did you say Alice *Tuckfield?*" At Geoffrey's nod, the master pushed his hair back from his face with an unsteady hand. "Sweet *Jesus!*"

"That's right. Well, Pup knew who they were. And it was one of them who gave me the letter for the Dame — I recognized his voice."

The shocked expression on Master Kenton's face was suddenly replaced by cynicism. He raised an eyebrow. "You really had me going there for a minute, Geoffrey. You recognized his voice, eh?" His tone was heavily sarcastic. "That's the proverbial last straw. Now run along."

"Master Kenton, I'm not playing a game," Geoffrey said, his face pale and intense. "Pup really was kidnapped last night, somewhere between the Bedern and

Dame Agnes's. *Please!* You *must* help us find her."

"Now see here, Geoffrey. If Pup really is a girl, much less Alice Tuckfield, do you really think Master Hunnis would have lied to me so she could go on singing in the choir? He would hardly think it proper."

Randall spoke up. "But you know how persuasive Pup can be. 'Please, sir, don't tell them. I like it here so much,' she'd say. And she really *is* gifted. Master Hunnis would know that." He shrugged. "Would *you* have betrayed her?"

"I am not William Hunnis," he said firmly.

"Maybe he thought she was safer here," he persisted. "There could be lots of reasons."

"Oh, I wish it *were* just a prank," Orlando blurted desperately. "Then we could all go home and laugh about it — with Pup." He bit his lips together hard, but one tear escaped anyway.

Master Kenton studied each of them in turn for a long moment, then shook his head. "I may be the most gullible fool in England, but I fear I'm beginning to believe you. But Geoffrey, whatever made you think you could recognize a voice you only heard once?"

"It was that on top of everything else," Geoffrey explained. "I kept telling myself I was being fanciful, especially after all Pup had told me. But then, when I got to the Dame's, Pup was gone, and the letter was about her — *and* the man rode away alone after he'd given me the letter."

"But why would they bother with a letter at all?"

Master Kenton mused. "A needless risk if they were just going to —" He fell silent.

"Maybe Pup told them Master Hunnis knows who she is or who they are," Randall suggested.

The master nodded. "And they need time to find out whether or not that was a bluff." He turned and faced the fire, drumming his fingers on the mantel shelf. A long moment passed. "Geoffrey," he said, "what exactly did Pup tell you? Did she tell you who the murderers are?"

"No. But she did tell me that Father Cooper is in league with them."

"Father *Cooper!*" he exclaimed. "Good Lord. No wonder Pup's so afraid of him." He shook his head angrily, then said decisively, "Come on. Let's go."

They leapt up.

"Where, sir?" Orlando asked eagerly.

"To Adrian's — Master Frost's." He pulled on his heavy greatcoat. "Are you *sure* Pup isn't with Nate?"

"I don't think so, sir," Randall said. "Nate left us before we left Pup — and she was headed in the opposite direction, last we saw her."

Suddenly, the master snapped his fingers. Delving into one deep pocket of his greatcoat, he produced a familiar green mitten. The boys gasped.

"I found this last night near the south door of the cathedral," he told them. "I guess that rules out Nate."

Geoffrey gulped, then nodded. "But one of us ought to get him, anyway. He'll help us."

Master Kenton nodded. "Very well. One of you run to Nate's and meet us at Master Frost's. He lives on Cooper Lane off Market Street."

"I'll go," Orlando volunteered, "as long as you promise to wait for me."

Master Kenton smiled ruefully. "No fear."

Orlando and Nate soon joined the others on the corner of Market Street and Cooper Lane. They were both out of breath and looked anxious.

Master Kenton raised one eyebrow. "Our last hope dashed, I see. I shudder to think what Adrian will say, but let's get it over with."

With Master Kenton leading the way, they strode up the steps of Master Frost's house and rapped on the door. There was no response for a long moment, then they heard footsteps and the door was flung open. Master Frost started to speak but stopped, staring at all the boys.

"Good Lord," he remarked at last, looking questioningly at Kenton. "Won't you step in?"

He took them into the parlor, where a good fire blazed on the hearth, and motioned them all to chairs. "I take it," he said, "that this isn't simply a social call. What is going on?"

Master Kenton outlined the happenings and their interpretation of them in a curt, clipped voice while Master Frost listened. "So now what, Adrian?" Kenton ended. "If Father Cooper is involved, shouldn't we go to the Dean?"

Master Frost sighed heavily, his brow knit with worry. Then he nodded. "I've been meaning to speak to Father Boyce about Pup since Hunnis's visit. Now I wish I had."

"Did William tell you something?" Kenton asked incredulously.

"Tell me? No. But I overheard them talking, so I knew — heaven forgive me — that Pup was a girl."

The boys gasped, and Kenton's jaw dropped.

"Well, good God, Hugh, what would you have had me do? It was too late to rearrange all the Christmas Eve music! And recess seemed the perfect time to deal with the problem, so I held my peace."

"I'm not blaming you, Adrian," Kenton said. "I'd have done the same in your shoes — though I'm not sure I'd have found the resolve to go to the Dean at all, in the end. But now it's a question of Pup's safety."

"Yes," Master Frost agreed. He turned to the boys. "Perhaps one of you had better go and reassure Dame Agnes. She's bound to be worried."

"But sir," Geoffrey protested, "she believed the letter. We didn't even *try* to explain to her. And we're often out all day."

Master Frost shrugged. "Very well, then. Come along."

When they arrived at the Deanery, Father Boyce received them in his second-floor study. If he was surprised by their visit, he gave no sign; he graciously offered to listen to whatever was troubling them.

"Father Boyce," Master Kenton began, "we have reason to believe one of the choristers has been kidnapped."

He stared at them. "Kidnapped? Who? And why?"

"Pup."

The Dean raised his eyebrows. "Well, go on."

"Pup is . . . Pup isn't . . . Pup's real name is —"

"Tucker, isn't it?" the Dean put in.

"No, Father," Kenton said, taking a deep breath. "It's Tuckfield."

"*Tuckfield?*" he thundered. "*Alice* Tuckfield? Sweet Jesus! Do you mean to tell me she's been in the choir for two *months?* Who knew?"

Geoffrey swallowed hard. "I, I think I was the only one who knew — or believed — she was Alice Tuckfield, but several of us knew she was a girl. We thought it would be a grand prank to hide her in the choir."

"A prank," the Dean repeated dully, resting his head in his hands. Suddenly he raised his head and looked keenly at Master Kenton. "You said 'kidnapped,' Hugh. Why?"

Briefly, Kenton explained about the letter and Master Hunnis's visit. The Dean listened, the bleak expression easing out of his face.

"She's no fool," he said finally. "But why, in the name of our Savior, didn't Hunnis *tell* me . . ."

"Pup said the Queen was involved," Geoffrey said. "Perhaps Master Hunnis thought —"

The Dean cut him off. "That's nonsense. Her Majesty would never have sanctioned Tuckfield's murder. Hunnis would know that."

"He probably felt Pup would be safer disguised as a boy," Master Kenton suggested.

Father Boyce nodded. He laced his fingers together and gazed down at them thoughtfully.

"Father Boyce!" Geoffrey blurted suddenly. "We forgot to tell you something. Pup said Father Cooper was involved in the conspiracy."

"Father Cooper? I can't believe that —" He stopped as he remembered his conversation with Pup. " 'Tell people the child is mad,' " he murmured. "They were talking about *her*. But then —"

"I know you'd rather not believe it," Kenton said, "but even I have seen how afraid Pup is of him."

"I'm sure she believes he's implicated, but she can't be right. He's a priest."

"He's a pompous, self-righteous, *ambitious* bag of wind," Kenton said acidly, "and you know it."

The boys gasped and the Dean glared angrily at the master. "See here, Kenton. I know you don't like the man, but *murder* . . . I can't believe he'd do it."

"He didn't do it," Geoffrey pointed out. "He planned it."

"That man wants to be a bishop so badly you can smell it on him." Kenton said sharply. "Perhaps he wouldn't do *anything* for a bishopric, but I shouldn't think he'd stop at much."

The Dean studied Kenton for a long moment. In

the silence, the ticking of the clock seemed deep and loud. Finally he sighed. "All right, I hear your words, but I can't accept it — not without some proof. I'm afraid I shall have to confront Father Cooper, try to satisfy myself as to whether he's involved or not."

"What good will it do?" Kenton demanded. "He's bound to deny it, and it will show our hand."

Father Boyce sighed. "I hope to set my own mind at rest, Kenton. Before I accuse my own Sub-Dean of murder, I need to be sure in my heart. Leave me now and come back" — he consulted the clock — "at one o'clock. Perhaps by then I'll have some news."

"But what should *we* do while we're waiting?" Geoffrey asked, unable to contain himself.

"I think you'd better go explain the situation to Dame Agnes." The Dean suppressed a smile at their expressions. "And Kenton, you should go with them. Make sure she understands they are not at fault and not to be punished."

Kenton shot a venomous look at him, which the Dean returned blandly. The organist turned on his heel and stalked to the door, trailing the boys and Master Frost in his wake. Father Boyce watched them go, shaking his head slightly. Then he reached for the bell pull and gave it a smart tug. A liveried footman appeared.

"My cloak, please, Hector. I'm going out."

"Why, Father Boyce!" Father Cooper exclaimed as he ushered the Dean into his parlor. "What a surprise —

and an honor. Do sit down. May I offer you some refreshment? Mulled wine, or some tea, perhaps?"

"No. No, thank you. I can't stay long. Dunstan, we're all quite concerned. Alister Tucker — Pup — has disappeared. You wouldn't know of any friends the boy might have in the city?"

Father Cooper shook his head. "I'm afraid I can't be of any help to you. But surely the lad is with one of the other choristers. After all, he can't have vanished."

The Dean studied his hands. "He isn't with any of the other boys, nor does Kenton have any idea where the boy might be. I'm rather afraid young Pup's been kidnapped." As he said the last word, he raised his eyes to Father Cooper's face in time to surprise a guilty start quickly smoothed over.

"Surely not," the priest said. "What use could a kidnapper have for a scruffy choirboy?"

"Adrian would have it that the boy was stolen by a rival choirmaster, but I'm not so sure."

"It does seem a bit . . . farfetched," Father Cooper agreed.

"Yes. And while I can't think of a single reasonable motive for kidnapping a mere chorister" — he fixed Father Cooper with an intent gaze — "I can think of at least one for kidnapping Alice Tuckfield."

The priest blenched but recovered quickly. "A non sequitur, surely?"

"Return the child, Dunstan, and I'll see that you get away to France before the hue and cry is raised."

Father Cooper shrugged eloquently. "I haven't the

faintest idea what you are talking about, Father. If the notion weren't completely preposterous, I'd almost think you were accusing *me* of kidnapping the poor child."

"I *am* accusing you," the Dean said, his voice icy. "I have it on reasonable authority that you are implicated in the murder of Sir Henry Tuckfield. Given that information, it's logical that you would want the child to disappear."

Father Cooper huffed. "I hardly think your absurd allegations constitute a conviction."

The Dean rose. "I warn you, Dunstan. I shall see you stripped of your orders, degraded from the priesthood, and punished with the strictest sentence the law will mete out!"

Father Cooper's smile was almost smug. "A jury must first convict me."

Without another word, the Dean strode to the door and went out, slamming it behind him.

CHAPTER SIXTEEN

When Alice awoke again, it was light in her prison. She was cramped and hungry, her head and throat ached awfully, but she was alive. That, she thought, was a start. Now, what to do?

With a great deal of effort, she managed to get into a sitting position and look around. The room was completely bare of any furniture other than the small brazier Father Cooper had brought. The walls were stone, and the windows were arched and slatted with horizontal boards. She knit her brow: where *could* she be? From her sitting position she could see the trap door in the floor; now, she thought, if only she could get her hands and legs free . . . and get rid of the horrible gag . . . She looked around the room for something sharp she could use as a tool, but there was nothing except the brazier and the bag of wood. The *brazier!* She worked her way carefully over to it. The fire had died down to a few sullen embers, but the metal sides were still fairly warm — too warm for her to touch comfortably. Perhaps, *perhaps* it would work.

Moving gingerly, she turned around. Carefully, she put her wrists and the rope that bound them against the rim and rubbed the cord back and forth. It hurt. The rim was not red hot, but it was hot all the same, and the metal was rather rough. The operation was further complicated by her inability to see what she was doing. But, before she reached the point where she couldn't bear it any longer, she felt the cord begin to give. She wrenched her wrists hard; the cord bit painfully into her sore arms, but the rope broke. As soon as her hands had recovered their feeling, she worked the gag off, then started on the ropes binding her legs.

Father Cooper had done his work well, Alice found. With her fingers so stiff and cold, she could not untie the knots. She could have screamed with frustration — except it hurt her throat too much. Finally, though, she managed to get to her feet, and by hopping awkwardly she made her way to the trap door.

She couldn't budge it. Father Cooper must have fastened it from the outside.

"*Blast!*" she croaked hoarsely. "Blast, blast, *blast!*"

Well, if she couldn't get out, perhaps she could call attention to herself in some way. Geoffrey must have figured out what happened to her by now; he would be looking for her — and probably with the others. She made her way to the windows and began trying to work loose one of the slats.

She would never have succeeded, except that some

of the wood was rotten. She managed to pry and break two slats apart enough so that she could see out. What she saw made her gasp.

She was in a tower — one of the cathedral towers — and it was a long way down. She now understood why Father Cooper had said no outcry would do any good. Even if she weren't so hoarse, she realized, she could never have made anyone on the ground hear her. How could she get anyone to notice her? she wondered.

"What I need is a banner," she said to herself; but the blanket was a ratty gray — not bright enough to show up against the stone — and she was dressed in shades of brown. The only thing of any color she had was her other mitten, and that was far too small. She sighed, then shivered. The room hadn't been warm to start with, and the opening in the window was making it worse. Perhaps she could coax a fire to life in the brazier; the wood was there, anyway.

She did manage to get a fire going at last, and the bright flames gave her the best idea she'd had so far. If she could get a piece of wood burning, she might be able to use it like a torch — if the wind didn't blow it out. It wouldn't be very visible in the daylight, but at *night* someone might see it. Of course, Father Cooper would probably come back before then — and he would tie her up again.

Finally, because she couldn't think of anything better to do, she took her remaining mitten, put a piece of wood into it to give it some weight, and dropped it out of the window. Maybe someone would see it fall, or maybe Geoffrey or one of the others would find it and put two and two together. Or maybe it wouldn't do any good at all . . . but a single mitten wasn't much use.

As she watched the piece of wood and the mitten fall, another idea came to her. She struggled back to the bag of wood and began pawing through it. At last she found what she was looking for: a piece of wood that fit her hands well enough to be used as a club. Maybe, if she were lucky and Father Cooper were careless, she could bludgeon him with it when he came back to feed her . . . if he came back. She took a position where she hoped she would not be immediately visible and settled down to wait.

"I apologize for troubling you, Dame Agnes," Kenton began, "but I fear there's no help for it."

The Dame took her cue from his grim tone and looked at the boys reproachfully. "*Now* what have you rascals been up to. Don't you know better than to bother poor Master Kenton with your naughtiness?" She looked up at the organist coyly. "Whatever have they been doing, dear Master Kenton?"

"I think Geoffrey had better explain."

Geoffrey opened his mouth to protest but thought better of it at the look Kenton gave him. "It's a long story. It all began about two months ago when Nate and I met a girl named Alice Tuckfield on the street. I knocked her down by mistake, and it came out that she hadn't anywhere to go, so we brought her here.

We gave her supper and let her sleep in the cupboard on the third floor."

The Dame drew a sharp breath but did not speak.

"Well, to make the tale shorter, we found out she could sing, and it was my idea to cut her hair and hide her in the choir. We didn't think old Fr — Master Frost would notice one new face, and we thought it would be a grand lark. He did notice her after about a week, but he didn't know she wasn't a boy, so he let her in. I'm talking about Pup, Dame Agnes."

The Dame put both her fists on her hips and leveled a steely glare at Geoffrey. *"Pup* is a girl? You can't be serious." He nodded solemnly. "Do you mean to tell me there's been a girl in this house for two months! Geoffrey Fisher, how *could* you? I knew you to be wretched little scamp, but I had no idea you were so lost to propriety as this! You had the audacity to foist some hoydenish brat on me and Master Frost? Didn't it ever occur to you that you sing in the *cathedral choir?* This is sacrilege! And *improper!* I knew you didn't have *much* in the way of any common decency, but this, *this* takes the bacon! Why —"

"That's not all, Dame Agnes," Randall interjected.

"It certainly isn't," she shrilled. "I've barely begun, young man! I'll —"

"Pup's been *kidnapped,*" Orlando cut in.

The Dame sat down abruptly. "What? *Why?* But the uncle —"

"Not her uncle," Geoffrey asserted. "It was a ploy to keep you from raising the hunt for Pup."

The Dame rounded on Master Kenton. "Is this true? Or is this some elaborate prank they've hoodwinked you into?"

"I only wish it were a prank," he told her. "Father Boyce sent me along to make sure you believed the boys and to tell you there's no need for you to punish them — he's taken that matter in hand."

"What's being done to find Pup?" the Dame asked, concern in her voice.

"The Dean has taken that matter in hand as well," he told her. "We are supposed to return to the Deanery later. We will certainly keep you informed of any developments."

The Dame looked from the boys to the master and back again. "I think," she said at last, "you'd better tell me the story from the beginning."

The meeting with the Dean was completely frustrating. He didn't have any news; furthermore, he utterly forbade the boys to take action of any kind. He told them that he had sent for the sheriff, and he indicated that he believed it likely that Father Cooper was in fact involved. Finally, he dismissed them, though he asked Master Frost to stay in case the sheriff had any questions for him.

Once the boys and Master Kenton were out in the street, Orlando spoke up gloomily.

"My father says that the only thing that grinds along slower than the mills of God is the authorities — and they don't grind as fine, either."

"If we wait for them to find Pup . . ." Nate was unable to finish the thought.

"I've half a mind to tail Father Cooper, Dean or no," Geoffrey muttered.

Randall looked unhappy. "I feel so helpless, and I can't quite shake the fear we're too late already."

"Use your head!" Master Kenton snapped. "Why bother with the letter, if they don't need time? They need to find Hunnis — that means London. On horseback, that's" — he shrugged — "three days, maybe more with the snow."

"Or less if he changes horses often and doesn't sleep much," put in Nate gloomily.

"Call it three days. Once he's in London, there's no guarantee Hunnis is there. He spent Christmas in — Kirbymoorside, was it?"

"But sir, that's not very far away at all. What if they're just going there?"

"They wouldn't have bothered with the letter, then," Kenton replied calmly.

"Will they murder Master Hunnis, do you think?" Geoffrey asked in a hushed tone.

Master Kenton frowned. "I don't believe they'll try it — too risky. I think they believe Pup's bluffing, but they don't quite dare to proceed with their plans until they know for certain."

"Is she, sir?" Nate asked.

He shrugged. "It doesn't matter. We'll find her before they have word from London one way or the other."

"We'll find her?" Orlando said. "You mean us? But how? You heard the Dean.

"Devil take the Dean!"

"Hooray!" Geoffrey crowed. "But how shall we work the night watch? I can sneak out — Gram's a heavy sleeper — and you can fix things with the Dame for Orlando, can't you, sir?"

"Now, wait just a minute!" Master Kenton said, spreading his hands. "If you all just keep an eye on Father Cooper during the day, I'll take the night watch."

"That's not fair!" Geoffrey protested. "You know he's more likely to be taking food to Pup at night. Besides, you shouldn't be on guard all alone, sir. What if he sees you?"

"I think I'm a match for that bag of wind," Kenton said grimly. "Don't argue with me. This isn't a game, Geoffrey. There's no question of fair or unfair."

"But it's stupid to take foolish risks! Suppose he gave you the slip? We might lose our chance of finding Pup."

"Geoffrey."

Geoffrey subsided reluctantly.

"Where do you suppose Father Cooper is now?" Nate asked.

"We can start looking at the cathedral," Randall said. "If he isn't there, we can go to his house."

"And knock on his door and inquire whether he's home? Use your head, Randall," Geoffrey said tartly.

"It's Father C's day for Evensong, isn't it?"

Master Kenton nodded.

"Then I recommend we each go home and make up excuses to miss dinner. And you," he added to Master Kenton, "can go home and have a nap if you're going to insist on having your way. You mustn't fall asleep, after all."

"Thank you, Geoffrey," Kenton said sarcastically. "I think I can manage to stay awake without a nap. But other than that, your plan has some merit. Orlando, I'll go along with you. I think I can manage the Dame for you."

Geoffrey laughed. "You could make her eat out of your hand, if you'd a mind to."

A little before Evensong, the four boys met on the south steps of the cathedral.

"Now that we're all here, let's go in," Orlando suggested. "There's no sense in standing around like cows in the rain."

"Wait a minute. I've been thinking," Nate said. "Won't Father Cooper think it odd that we're all at Evensong?"

"He won't notice us," Geoffrey said confidently.

"Well, maybe not," Randall put in, "but ol' Frost might, and he'd know we were up to something."

"But if we can't go in, how can we watch Father Cooper?" Orlando asked. "I think we'll just have to take our chances."

"No. I thought it all out," Nate said. "We can watch

from the triforium. If we're careful, no one will see us."

"Oh, good job, Nate," Geoffrey said. "Let's go."

"You know," Geoffrey whispered, when they had found a place with a good view of both the lectern and the sacristy door, "I've been thinking, too. It's foolhardy of Kenton to want to tackle Father Cooper alone, so I told my Gram I'd be at your house overnight, Nate."

Nate gasped. "And she believed you? It must be nice."

"Well, I'm not sure she did, actually. She's pretty cagey. But all she did was look at me rather oddly and say, 'Well, boys will be boys, I suppose.'"

Randall shook his head. "My mother subjected me to a positive inquisition. How did you and Sourface make out with the Dame, Orlando?"

He grinned. "I've never seen anything like it! Dame Agnes smiled and nodded and poured tea. Master Kenton could have told her anything — he could have told her he was taking me to the *knackers* to be made into glue and she'd have agreed to it. Nothing could have been easier."

At that moment, Master Kenton began the prelude and the boys broke off their conversation. When the service was over, Father Cooper went into the sacristy to take off his vestments. The boys watched the door like cats at a mousehole. Finally the priest emerged, wrapped in a cloak, and set off at a brisk pace toward the west end of the cathedral. The boys hurried quietly along the triforium, keeping him in sight.

"Sprint ahead, Orlando, and go down the stairs," Geoffrey advised. "We don't want to lose him."

The boys watched from the doorway as Father Cooper started down the steps and across the close toward his house on Precentors Lane. He hadn't gone very far when he stooped down and picked something up off the ground. Then he turned back toward the boys. They melted into the shadows of the doorway as quickly as they could, but the priest didn't seem to notice them. He was looking up, at the roof or the towers, with a frown on his face. Finally, he turned around and started off briskly for home.

"That was *close!*" Geoffrey breathed deeply. "Come on."

They followed the priest from a discreet distance and arrived at his house in time to see him disappear inside. They sheltered in an adjacent doorway to take counsel.

"The old tub of lard is probably sitting down to dinner," Orlando said. "I wish we could join him. I'm hungry."

"There must be a back door," Randall said. "Someone ought to watch it."

"I'll go," Nate volunteered. "Want to come, Geoffrey?"

Geoffrey displayed some coins triumphantly. "I'm going to trot down to the White Hart and get us some meat pasties."

"Blessed Geoffrey!" Randall laughed. "You think of everything."

A few minutes later, when Geoffrey returned, only Orlando was watching the front of the house.

"Randall went to check on Nate," he explained. "Listen, Geoffrey. Shall I sneak out and join you tonight? It would be easy, once the Dame's in bed."

"If you're caught, it'll mean a beating," Geoffrey warned.

"Do you think you're the only one willing to risk a beating for Pup's sake?" he demanded hotly.

Geoffrey grinned and clapped Orlando on the back. "I'm glad I'm not. It'll be nice to have company, Orlando. But I'd better take these pasties around to Randall and Nate before they're stone cold."

An hour passed slowly, marked by the tolling of the cathedral bell. Nothing happened. The boys were cold and cramped from crouching in the shadows. Randall came around to the front to confer with Geoffrey and Orlando.

"It's getting late," he said. "Maybe we should send someone off to get Master Kenton. My mother will start to worry if I'm not home soon."

Before Geoffrey could reply, they heard the front door open. Shrinking into the shadows, they watched Father Cooper descend the steps. They held perfectly still, barely daring to breathe, as he passed their hiding place and continued down the street.

"Quick, Randall," Geoffrey whispered. "Get Nate while we start after him."

Cautiously, they followed Father Cooper. He led them through the streets to the cathedral and disappeared inside. The boys hesitated; then Geoffrey carefully eased the door open a crack and peered inside. The priest had lit a lantern. Geoffrey could see the light bobbing along, half the nave away. He opened the door further and slipped inside, motioning for the others to follow.

"Split up," Geoffrey breathed. "Follow from the aisle and the triforium. If he sees one of us, someone go for Kenton."

They nodded as they scattered on silent feet. Geoffrey went softly up the center of the nave, keeping Father Cooper's light in sight. The priest turned into the sacristy. Geoffrey crept to the door, straining his ears. He could hear the priest moving about, opening cupboards. Geoffrey crouched down in the shadows behind a chair. The priest came back through the door carrying something, a silver ewer and, and . . . Geoffrey couldn't see clearly. He edged a little nearer. A cloth sack with — could it be a loaf of bread? He had to be sure. As he crept closer, his foot struck the leg of a chair, which scraped along the floor with a noise of thunder. The priest whirled about. Geoffrey had just time to register that it was in fact a loaf of bread before the priest swooped down on him like a falcon striking and hauled him to his feet by his hair.

CHAPTER SEVENTEEN

"Let go!" Geoffrey shrieked, thinking *that* ought to warn the others. "You're hurting me!" Then he looked up into Father Cooper's face, and his heart seemed to stop with horror. He had never seen anyone look so angry. The priest's face was almost perfectly white, his eyes blazing. Geoffrey swallowed hard.

"Geoffrey!" Father Cooper said, tightening his grip. "And what are you doing in the cathedral at this hour?"

"Playing hide-and-seek, Father," he replied, hoping fervently that his voice was carrying to the others.

His eyes narrowed and a faint, sarcastic smile touched his lips. "How apt: I'm It, and you've just been put out of the game."

"No, sir," Geoffrey said with as much puzzled innocence as he could manage. "*Randall's* It. Please let go of my hair."

Geoffrey saw a shade of doubt touch the priest's

face. "*Randall's* It?" he repeated. "And who else is playing?"

"Nate," he answered. Orlando was the fleetest runner.

"Really?" There was still disbelief in his voice.

"Nate! Randall! Allie-allie-in-come-free!" he shouted.

Orlando took his cue and began to creep toward the door. As he went, he heard scuffling and footsteps from the others.

"And I had the best hiding place," Nate grumbled sullenly.

Father Cooper eyed Geoffrey inscrutably while the others assembled. Then he turned to Randall, looking very pained.

"Randall, I confess I'm surprised at you. Hide-and-seek in the cathedral? I thought you had more feeling for the reverence due a house of God."

"But it's perfect for hide-and-seek," Geoffrey put in unrepentantly, "especially in the dark."

"I didn't say I was surprised at *you*. Everyone knows what a lamentably irreverent, impertinent and impossible little beast you are, but I didn't think even *you* could lead Randall astray."

By then Orlando had reached the door. He eased it open, slipped out into the night, and ran for all he was worth. He arrived at Master Kenton's, panting, and knocked on the door. Kenton opened it at once.

"I was wondering when you'd come. What's wrong?"

"Father Cooper caught Geoffrey in the cathedral," Orlando gasped. "Geoffrey said — said he was playing hide-and-seek."

"Quick thinking. Did Father Cooper believe him?"

"I think so. But he won't if they don't go home when he tells them to. If we don't want to lose Father Cooper, we'd better hurry."

Kenton put on his cloak and the muffler and came outside. "Where was Geoffrey caught?" he asked as they loped toward the cathedral.

"By the sacristy door."

"Then we'll go in by the south door. If they're still there, Father Cooper won't see us come in."

When they arrived at the cathedral, they were relieved to hear Father Cooper still haranguing. "Up," Orlando mouthed, motioning toward the stair to the triforium. They groped their way in the dark.

"— this impertinence that borders on sacrilege —"

"We didn't do any harm!" Geoffrey protested.

"I've had more than enough of your impudence, young man. Rest assured that I shall report this incident — and most particularly your insolent attitude, Geoffrey Fisher! — to the Dean. Father Boyce shall see you severely punished."

"Do you have to report it to the Dean, Father?" Randall asked in a chastened tone. "It won't happen again, and we're very sorry."

"I'm not!" Geoffrey put in.

"Geoffrey, *please* be quiet," Nate said. "It's bad enough already."

"Indeed, it is bad enough already," Father Cooper said. "*Worse* than bad enough. Now, you should all go home and leave me to my prayers. There is something very wrong when a man of God finds the sanctity and peace of the cathedral itself destroyed by rowdy and irreverent games. Now go!"

They went.

"I wonder if Orlando and Kenton made it in time?" Randall asked once they were outside.

"They had to," Nate said. "He sure yelled long enough."

"We can't take any chances," Geoffrey said firmly. "Do you know what he fetched out of the sacristy? Food. I'm going back in."

"If he catches you now, he's sure to smell a rat," Randall said softly.

Geoffrey nodded and started toward the south door. Nate watched him go. "Shouldn't we go with him?" he asked.

Randall shook his head. "Three are noisier than one. I think we should wait for a few minutes in case Orlando and Master Kenton haven't arrived yet. Then we'd better go home. My mother's going to flay me."

Inside the cathedral, Geoffrey could see the light from Father Cooper's lantern, still by the sacristy; he could hear the priest moving about. Cautiously, Geoffrey groped his way up to the triforium — and nearly collided with Kenton and Orlando.

"Bravely played," Master Kenton breathed. "But now, both of you go home. I'll watch."

Before either boy could respond, the priest picked up the lantern and the sack and started down the nave. Kenton moved stealthily to the staircase and descended. Geoffrey and Orlando made no move, but stayed and watched from the triforium. Father Cooper padded down the center of the nave, then turned and headed for the south aisle. If Geoffrey strained his eyes, he thought he could make out Kenton's dark figure following. The priest made for the stairway that led to the crypt. Orlando clutched Geoffrey's arm in excitement, and Geoffrey put one hand over his own mouth and held his breath. Father Cooper vanished into the dark stairway; then, suddenly, the beam of the lantern swung about, catching Kenton squarely. With surprising agility, Father Cooper launched himself at Master Kenton.

Geoffrey saw it first — the glint of light on the heavy gilded crucifix in the priest's hand — but the movement was too swift for him to cry out in warning. Father Cooper swung his arm and brought his hand down on the back of Kenton's head with a sickening thud. The master crumpled. Then the priest knelt down swiftly, reaching for Kenton's throat.

"Murder!" Orlando screamed. *"Murder! Murder!"*

Father Cooper scrambled to his feet and fled, leaving the lantern behind him.

CHAPTER EIGHTEEN

Geoffrey and Orlando pelted down the stairs and up the aisle. Kenton lay very still, sprawled awkwardly across the aisle. Together, the two boys managed to turn him over onto his back. Orlando put his ear against the man's chest.

"He's alive," he said. "Geoffrey, get some water."

Geoffrey picked up the ewer. "There's water in thi. What do I do? Dump it on him?"

"Just a little of it."

Geoffrey dribbled some water onto the master's face while Orlando shook him gently. "Please, Master Kenton, please wake up."

For an interminable time, nothing happened; at last his eyes fluttered open. He groaned and sat up.

"What happened?" he asked thickly.

"You got knocked on the head," Geoffrey told him. "We thought you were dead."

"Sorry to disappoint you. What are you doing here, anyway? I thought I told you to go home."

"Well, we thought you might be glad of our company," Orlando said tartly. "We'll go away if you like. Then Father Cooper can come back and finish his botched job."

He raised a hand as if acknowledging a hit. "Very well. Say 'I told you so' and get it over with. Then maybe you'll help me up." He put a hand gingerly to the back of his head. "What on earth did he hit me with?"

"It looked like a crucifix, sir," Geoffrey said. "Come on. We'd better find Pup."

They helped Kenton to his feet. He swayed and leaned on Geoffrey's shoulder. "I'm as weak as watered ale," he said with disgust. "But I'll do as long as we don't go too fast. Any ideas of where to start?"

"The crypt!" The boys said together.

"Very well. Let's go. Orlando, take the lantern, and Geoffrey, bring the sack of food."

Orlando looked at Master Kenton's pale face doubtfully. "Are you sure you don't want to wait for us here, sir?"

"Yes!" he snapped. "I'll be all right if we take it slowly."

Carefully, they descended the stairs. Orlando stayed behind to help Master Kenton, but when they reached the bottom, Geoffrey hurried forward to the grille.

"It's locked!" he called out, grabbing the bars and

rattling them in frustration. "The verger has the key."

"The verger won't like being woken up," Orlando said.

"I weep for the verger," Geoffrey retorted.

"Just wait a minute," Kenton said, groping around on the wall above his head. His fingers found the ledge he sought, and triumphantly he produced a large, ornate brass key. He gave it to Geoffrey, who fitted it into the lock.

"Oh, clever!" Geoffrey said enthusiastically as the gate swung open. "How'd you know about that, Master Kenton?"

He shrugged. "The verger showed me. Now I suppose he'll have to find another hiding place to be safe from you rascals."

They went in and searched the place quickly. There was no sign of her.

"Now what?" Orlando asked.

"Let's go upstairs and think about it," Geoffrey suggested. "It's creepy down here."

Back in the nave, Kenton sat down on a chair and looked at each of the boys. His face was pale and drawn.

"We can't even be sure Pup's in the cathedral," he said wearily.

"She must be," Geoffrey insisted. "Otherwise, why keep food for her here? It would make more sense to keep food in his own kitchen if she were somewhere else, wouldn't it?"

"You have a point," the master acknowledged.

"But if he's keeping her in the cathedral, it would have to be a place that isn't used very often, like the crypt," Orlando put in.

"Have you been all around the triforium?" Kenton asked.

Both boys jumped up. "No."

The master began to struggle to his feet.

"We'll be much quicker if you wait for us," Geoffrey pointed out.

He smiled ruefully and sat back down. "Then hurry."

When they returned, Kenton took one look at their faces and gave a heavy sigh. "Not there. Where else could he have put her?"

"I don't know," Orlando began. "Maybe the Chapter House —"

"No! The tower!" Geoffrey interrupted. "That's it!"

"The bell tower?" Kenton asked. "But someone goes up there every hour, Geoffrey."

"Not the bell tower. The other tower. The north tower. The empty tower! Remember, Orlando, how Father Cooper looked up at it on his way home?"

Orlando struck his fist into his open palm. "You've got it! It must be that. Let's go!" He looked doubtfully at Master Kenton. "Are you —"

"Yes!" Kenton flared. "Stop fussing."

They climbed flight upon flight of stairs, stopping frequently to rest. At last they reached the end of the stairs. The chamber was empty. Orlando groaned,

Kenton cursed under his breath, and Geoffrey looked around in disbelief.

"Hold the lantern up higher, Orlando," he ordered.

Mystified, Orlando obeyed.

"But it *has* to be," Geoffrey murmured, shaking his head. Then he looked up at the ceiling. He took the lantern out of Orlando's hand and shined the light up.

"A trap door!" they exclaimed together.

"Yes, but how are we getting up there?" Kenton asked. "Do you little angels have wings?"

Geoffrey paid no attention. He was scanning the walls again, searching for something. He gave a small sigh of satisfaction, went to one of the walls, and loosed a slender cord from a cleat on the wall. As if by magic, a rope ladder unrolled from the ceiling.

"Bravo, Geoffrey!" Orlando cried.

"Well, well," Kenton said. "How did you know about that, young Geoffrey?"

"There's one just like it in the other tower, to get up into the belfry. I made friends with one of the ringers last year." Then he climbed nimbly up and set his shoulder to the trap door. It wouldn't budge.

"I can't open it," he called down to the others.

On the other side of the trap door, Alice dropped her billet of wood with a resounding thud. *"Geoffrey!"* she tried to shout, but she knew he'd never hear her with her voice so hoarse. Instead, she beat frantically on the door with the wood.

"Pup!" three voices shouted at once.

"There must be a latch, Geoffrey," Master Kenton advised. "Orlando, take him the lantern."

"Got it," Geoffrey cried as his fingers found the bolt and threw it back. He pounded a couple of times to warn Pup to get off the door, then put his shoulder to it again. This time it opened with a reluctant groan. Geoffrey sprang into the room.

"Pup!" he shouted, giving her a fierce hug. "Oh, Pup, I've been so *worried!*"

"For God's sake, Geoffrey," Master Kenton called up irritably, "is she all right? Bring her down!"

"My legs are still tied," Alice told Geoffrey. "Have you got a knife?" Then her expression changed suddenly. "*Her?* Geoffrey, did you tell him?"

He nodded. "I had to. I —"

"Oh, it's all right, I understand," she assured him hurriedly. "Knife?"

Geoffrey fished in his pocket, pulled out his knife, and a moment later they were both down the ladder. Orlando hugged her almost before her feet had touched the floor; then Master Kenton took her by the shoulders and looked down at her. She looked up at him anxiously.

"You're not angry, are you, Master?" she whispered.

He pulled her into an awkward hug. "No, I'm not angry," he said, his voice strangely tight, "but I think we had better go. I doubt we fooled Father Boyce. He's probably waiting up for us."

"Will he be *very* angry?" Orlando asked a little anxiously.

"When we bring him Pup?" Kenton retorted.

"Does Father Boyce know about me too, then?" Alice asked.

Master Kenton nodded.

"What will happen to me now?" A quaver crept into her voice.

"Time enough to worry about that in the morning," Master Kenton said briskly. "Now do you think you can walk, or shall I carry you?"

"I can walk if we take it slowly," she assured him.

They all went back to the Deanery. When they pounded on the door with the heavy knocker. it was opened almost immediately by a footman, who turned to an underling with a murmured command and curt nod. A moment later, the Dean appeared. He looked them over anxiously and saw Alice leaning against Master Kenton.

"You found her! Praise God. Are you all right, Alice?"

She nodded.

Father Boyce turned to one of his servants. "Abram, show Miss Tuckfield to a guest room. Go on, child," he added to her. "You need your rest."

When the boys made to follow her, the Dean stopped them with a curt gesture. "*You* are coming with me," he told them sternly. "There are several very worried people you need to reassure." Suddenly he looked sharply at Master Kenton. "Are you all right?"

Kenton swayed on his feet and the Dean caught his arm to steady him.

"I'm just fine," he replied impatiently. "You're as bad as Orlando, trying to hound me into an early grave. I just lost a little argument with Father Cooper — nothing to fret over."

"Well, don't tell me now," the Dean advised. "You'll only have to repeat it for the others."

When they arrived in the Dean's upstairs parlor, they found Master Frost, Dame Agnes and Geoffrey's grandmother, Mistress MacLeod, all seated by the fire. As the Dean and the others entered, Master Frost stood up, relief on his face.

"Oh, thank God," he said. "Did you find Pup?"

They nodded.

"Is — is she all right?"

Kenton laughed. "It would take more than a brush with a kidnapper to upset *Pup*. She's fine, a little shaky on her feet, but, considering all she's been through, it's nothing short of remarkable."

"You look a little shaky yourself," Mistress MacLeod observed. "Did my rascally Geoffrey wear you out or is it something more serious?"

"He's hurt," Geoffrey said. "Father Cooper clouted him with a crucifix."

Orlando nodded. "Knocked him out."

The Dame found her voice. "Oh, you *poor* man!"

The Dean shook his head slowly. "Tell us the story from the beginning."

It fell to Geoffrey to relate the evening's events. He told the story without undue embellishment, aware all the time of the Dean's cool eyes on him. When he had finished, he remarked, "Won't Nate and Randall be *sick* with jealousy when they hear about all the excitement they missed."

"It sounds to me like they got a fair amount of excitement as it was," Master Frost pointed out, a smile tugging at the corners of his mouth.

"Well, it sounds to *me*," Father Boyce said sternly, "like you were all far, *far* luckier than you had any right to be. But it's late. I've had rooms prepared for all of you. The footman will show you. Go on, boys," he added sternly when they began to look rebellious.

"But Father Boyce, what will happen to Pup?" Geoffrey asked worriedly.

"We'll discuss that in the morning. Now, bed."

"*But* —"

"*Bed*," he said with menace.

Geoffrey sighed in defeat. "Goodnight."

"Goodnight," the others replied. Then Geoffrey's grandmother shepherded them out.

"How did you know to come looking for me, Gram?" Geoffrey asked as they went through the door.

Her brisk rejoinder was clearly audible. "Come, come, Geoffrey. I'm neither so old nor so deaf that I can't tell when you're fibbing. Stay at Nate's, indeed!"

CHAPTER NINETEEN

When Alice awoke the next morning, it took her some time to get her bearings. At first she couldn't understand what she was doing in this big, comfortable bed — such a far cry from her cot in the dormitory; then memory came rushing back. She wondered how Geoffrey had found her so quickly, and though she tried not to think about it, she wondered what the Dean would do with her now.

Her thoughts were interrupted by a gentle tap at the door.

"Come in," she called, and a servant entered carrying a covered tray.

"Here's your breakfast, Miss Tuckfield," he told her, setting the tray on the bedside table. "If there's anything else you need, just ring." He gestured to a tapestry bell pull on the wall.

"Thank you," she said to his retreating back.

Alice got up and went to the washstand. She poured

water from the pitcher into the basin and splashed her face. Her wrists looked raw and angry where the cord had bitten, but after she washed the cuts clean, she thought they felt a little better, and her fingers weren't as stiff. She dressed quickly before she investigated the breakfast tray. There was a pot of tea, a large slice of ham, some scrambled eggs and a helping of porridge. Alice hadn't realized how hungry she was. She ate every crumb.

When she was finished she sat for a moment, trying to decide whether to ring the bell and ask to see the Dean or to go in search of him on her own. Before she made up her mind, there was a knock on the door. She got up and opened it.

"Geoffrey! Orlando! Good morning."

"You look better today," Orlando observed. "Last night, you looked as motley as a molting bird. Are you feeling better?"

She nodded. "And I can almost talk normally," she added. "So tell me: what *happened?* How did you find me so quickly?"

"We're supposed to bring you to Father Boyce," Geoffrey told her, "but we can tell you on the way."

So they did. Alice listened avidly, her eyes clouding with concern when they told her about the attack on Master Kenton.

"He's all right, isn't he?" she asked anxiously.

"Oh yes," Orlando assured her. "His head is harder than a *dozen* crucifixes."

When Geoffrey knocked on the door of the Dean's

study, Pup felt her stomach give an alarming lurch. She hoped he wouldn't be angry with her for her deception, but she was afraid he would *never* understand. She took a deep breath to calm herself as she entered with the boys. Father Boyce looked up from his desk as they came in. He didn't look angry, she thought. He was even smiling.

"Good morning, Alice," he greeted her. "Before you ask, I've sent for Randall and Nate, so they can be reassured of the success of their endeavors. They should be arriving any minute now. In the meantime, I need to know what *you* think I should do with you. Of course, you realize I can't let you stay on in the choir, so what should I do?"

Alice bit her lip. "My father said I should go to Lady Jenny at Chellisford Hall, but I've never met her, and I don't know whether she'd want me."

The Dean raised his eyebrows. "Lady *Jenny?* Oh, Alice, I don't know . . ." He hesitated, and Alice's heart sank as it occurred to her that her father's friend might be considered as unconventional as Father himself had been. "I almost hate to ask her — she might feel she couldn't refuse," he added — tactfully, Alice thought.

"Well," Alice said in a small voice, "what did *you* have in mind, Father Boyce?"

The Dean studied Alice for a moment before he spoke. "My sister is the abbess of Saint Helen's. She could take you in, oversee your education, and see that you are treated in a manner suited to your rank."

"My *rank?*" Alice protested. "I don't care about my *rank.* Can't I just go and live with Mistress MacLeod? I'm sure she'd take me in."

"However you feel about it now, Alice, you are a noble's child and you should be raised accordingly."

"My father was a *musician,*" she said hotly. "He didn't care that he was also a knight. Father Boyce, I really don't want to go to Saint Helen's. It's a long way away and I don't have any friends there."

"You would make new friends," the Dean assured her. "You've made quite a few in the short time you've been here, you know."

"I know," she said, her throat suddenly tight. "And I don't want to go away and *leave* them all."

Father Boyce nodded. "I understand that. But you'll be able to come back for visits once in a while."

"If you had already made up your mind," Alice said angrily, "why did you even bother to ask me what I thought you should do with me?"

"Now, Alice," he began, but he was interrupted by knocking on the door. "Come in."

The door burst open and Nate and Randall raced into the room. "*Pup!*" they cried, hugging her.

"Thank *God* they found you!" Randall said.

"Yes, but what *happened* after we left?" Nate demanded. "And how did you get caught in the first place, Pup?"

"Yes, tell us!"

The Dean held up his hand for silence. "Do tell

them, Pup, but why don't you go to the library? I had Abram light the fire in there for you. If you'd like, I can send in some tea and cakes."

"Thank you, that would be nice," Randall said.

"It's the double doors at the end of this hallway," he told them.

After they had gone, Father Boyce rang his bell. When the servant appeared, he asked him to send Master Frost and Master Kenton in. They appeared a short time later, Master Kenton a little pale but steady enough. After greetings were exchanged and the men were seated, the Dean laced his fingers together and studied them for a moment.

"Gentlemen, I need your advice. I'm somewhat at a loss to know what to do with young Alice. I had thought to send her to my sister, who is the abbess at Saint Helen's. It seemed the perfect solution, but Alice is not enthusiastic."

"I can't say that I blame her," Master Frost said. "It seems to me that Pup is of far too lively a temperament to be happy in a contemplative way of life."

"Saint Helen's?" Kenton remarked. "That's near Liverpool, isn't it?"

Father Boyce nodded. "But, really, it could do her a great deal of good. They won't treat her badly, after all, and I really don't know what else to do with her."

There was a glint of sarcasm in Master Kenton's expression. "Such a *convenient* solution, too. Isn't that what convents are for?"

"Now Hugh." The Dean bristled. "I asked for your advice."

"Well, my advice is to think of something else."

"What, precisely, do you have in mind?" Father Boyce inquired icily.

"Perhaps Mistress MacLeod would take her in, or one of the other boys' families."

"That's hardly feasible," Father Boyce snapped. "She's a noble's daughter."

Anger flared in Kenton's eyes, but his next words were quiet, almost dispassionate. "Satisfy your idea of propriety however you must, but if you send Pup off to a convent, Father Boyce, I will resign."

"Hugh!" Master Frost gasped.

"Are you serious?" the Dean demanded.

"Perfectly," he replied levelly.

"But Hugh —" Father Boyce began, but Kenton's voice closed over his, implacable as the tide.

"After all Pup has been through, it's the worst kind of cruelty to send her away in disgrace."

"Who said anything about disgrace?" the Dean argued.

"How will it look to Pup?" Kenton asked; then he rose. "Find a place where she can be happy, Father Boyce. Good day." He strode to the door and went out, shutting it with more force than necessary. Master Frost and the Dean sat in silence. Then the Dean sighed.

"Adrian, what do I do about that?" he asked at last.

Master Frost shrugged. "Perhaps there is a noble family in York that would be willing to take Pup in."

"I've half a mind to call his bluff," he muttered.

"You will, of course, do as you think best," Master Frost replied a little stiffly, "though I, for one, don't believe Hugh is bluffing. It's not as if he couldn't find another place."

The Dean shook his head. "Well, perhaps there is someone who would take in the girl after all. At least I can try. I shall speak to our good patroness, Lady Genevieve Andrewes. Perhaps she can help."

Several hours later, in another wing of the Deanery, a footman ushered Lady Genevieve Andrewes into a drawing room. Father Boyce rose as she entered, pulling a chair up to the fire for her. She seated herself with a murmured word of thanks. The Dean ran a hand through his hair and cleared his throat.

"The reason I asked you to come to see me, my lady, is that I have a problem and I need some advice."

She nodded graciously.

"It's rather a delicate situation." He related Alice's tale while the lady listened impassively. "You must see that it is imperative that we find a place for her to stay. I thought you might have some suggestions."

"What of your sister's convent — Saint Helen's, isn't it? But surely you thought of that. It won't answer?"

"Well, no. You see, neither Frost nor Kenton think she'd be happy there, and Kenton feels strongly enough about it to threaten to resign unless some other solution is found."

Lady Genevieve Andrewes raised her eyebrows. "*Kenton* threatened to leave on the child's account? That's astounding. I didn't think he had a heart to be touched. The girl must be quite a charmer. It makes me curious to meet her. After all," she added with an odd, secretive smile, "Hal Tuckfield didn't go out of his way to be endearing."

"I wasn't personally acquainted with him," the Dean responded. "But it still leaves me with a problem."

"Indeed. Well, I'm sure some solution can be found that will keep the child in York."

"Frost did suggest that there might be a noble family in York that would be willing to take Alice Tuckfield in. I thought you might be able to recommend someone to me."

For a long moment she was silent, gazing into the fire. Then she turned her cool, gray eyes on the Dean. "I don't think you need to trouble yourself any further over this. I will be happy to take her in."

"But my lady," the Dean protested, "I wouldn't want to impose on you."

A smile lurked in her eyes. "You know I'd never permit *that*. You know how I feel about the school. Something must be done, and I am willing to do it. You may safely leave the details to me."

"Oh, but my lady, I'm sure I shouldn't let you put yourself to so much trouble," the Dean said.

"Nonsense, Edgar," she responded firmly.

"I can't tell you how grateful I am," he went on. "We are fortunate to have so kind a patroness."

"Spare my blushes," she replied. "I am delighted to be of assistance."

CHAPTER TWENTY

The next morning, the Dean again summoned Alice to his study. She tapped on the door, acutely aware of her thumping heart. The Dean greeted her with a smile.

"Well, I think you'll be pleased to learn that you are to be spared the convent."

Hope lit Alice's eyes. "You aren't sending me away?"

"No. You seem to have collected a surprising number of staunch supporters. Master Kenton threatened to resign if I sent you to Saint Helen's, so I have bowed to necessity." His eyes narrowed slightly. "You don't have a dress?" He sighed when she shook her head. "A pity, but it can't be helped. Lady Genevieve Andrewes will be here soon — she's our good patroness. You will be staying with her, at least for the moment."

"Oh," Alice said in a small voice. "Father Boyce, what is she like?"

He was silent, considering; finally he smiled. "She lives near York, so she must be better than Saint Helen's. She is . . . well, she is a very *good* woman, Pup. But you'll see for yourself quite soon."

His words sounded ominous to Alice. She bit her lip resolutely and nodded.

"Now, run along, child," he added. "I'll send someone to fetch you when she arrives."

Alice sketched something between a bow and a curtsy and left the chamber. She stopped in her room to get her music, paused to tell one of the footmen where she was going, then went over to the school to practice. On the way, she ran into Geoffrey.

"Hey, Pup! What's up?" he greeted her.

"I'm off to practice. I —" There was a catch in her voice. Geoffrey put his arm around her shoulders.

"Steady there! What's the matter?"

"They're sending me away."

Geoffrey gasped. "Not to Saint Helen's!"

"No, no," she assured him hurriedly. "I'm being sent to stay with Lady Andrewes."

He heaved a relieved sigh.

"Geoffrey," she asked him, "do you know the patroness? What's she like?"

He shook his head. "I've never met her, Pup. Didn't Father Boyce tell you anything?"

"He said she is a very *good* woman. Sounds dire, doesn't it? She's probably stuffy and proper and old. I will scandalize her, and she'll make me sew samplers all day." She sighed. "But at least I'll be nearby. I can always slip away and come to visit." Then her composure broke. "Geoffrey, can't I run away and stay with your gram?" she pleaded.

"I think Gram would say you have to give Lady Andrewes a chance." He tried a rallying tone. "You might even like her, Pup."

She sighed. "Pigs might fly, too. Well, I'm off to practice. See you later, Geoffrey."

"See you, Pup."

A few minutes later, Alice was settled at the virginal in the choir room. As she turned her attention to the music, her doubts and fears were forgotten. It wasn't until her stomach began reminding her it was lunchtime that she was recalled to her problems. Feeling somewhat more hopeful, she went back to the Deanery for lunch.

Later that afternoon, Father Boyce sent for Alice. As she stood outside the study door, she took a deep breath to steady herself, then knocked.

"Come in."

She opened the door. Father Boyce and Lady Genevieve Andrewes were standing by the fireplace.

"Ah, Alice, come meet Lady Genevieve."

As Alice approached the fire, the lady turned. Alice's eyes widened. She was not at all the way Alice had pictured her. Instead of the prim, gray-haired lady of her imagination, Alice found herself face to face with a young woman with cool gray eyes and light brown hair.

There was a hint of something — was it mischief? — in her expression as she nodded graciously at Alice.

"Lady Genevieve, Alice Tuckfield. Alice, Lady Genevieve Andrewes."

"I'm honored to make your acquaintance, my lady," Alice murmured.

Lady Genevieve nodded again, then turned to the Dean. "Do you think you could have her things sent along? I brought the sleigh, and there isn't much room."

"I haven't much, my lady," Alice said. "Just the things in my satchel."

She smiled at Alice. "There's certainly room for that, then, but don't you have books or things you want from your father's house — at least some more appropriate clothing?"

"Of course," Alice replied, feeling herself blush.

"Can you arrange it, Edgar?"

"Yes, indeed, my lady."

She inclined her head graciously. "Then I think we had better take our leave."

"My lady, I can't thank you enough," the Dean said. "You can't imagine what a relief it is to be able to rely so completely on you."

"I'm delighted to be of service." She reached down and took Alice's hand. "Come along, Miss Alice. Good day, Edgar."

Once they were outside in Lady Genevieve's sleigh, she turned to Alice. Her eyes were full of amusement.

"I saw your face, Alice — or may I call you Pup? What on *earth* did Edgar tell you about me that made you look so apprehensive and then so surprised?"

"He said you're a very *good* woman," Alice replied, rather taken aback by the abrupt change in Lady Genevieve's manner.

She burst out laughing. "Good God! You poor child! And you had visions of embroidering endless altarcloths and knitting mittens for the poor. But surely you — I mean, after all, didn't Hal ever mention me? He used to call me 'Wild Jenny'— or 'Jenny-Mule' when he was annoyed. You couldn't really have had any fears . . ." She trailed off in the face of Alice's bewildered expression.

"You knew my father?" she said. Then the bewilderment was swept aside by a rush of realization and relief. "You're Lady Jenny!"

"That's right," she said with a smile. "Not quite what you expected?"

Alice shook her head. "Master Frost and Father Boyce refer to you as 'our good patroness.' "

She gave a gasp of laughter. "Oh, heavens! Well, I promise you, Pup: no altarcloths! I don't even *own* an embroidery frame, shocking as that may be. Father Boyce described me as 'good' because he doesn't quite dare describe me as 'eccentric.' That's one of the advantages of being wealthy. Now tell me, Pup: do you want to continue your studies at the school?"

Alice's eyes widened. "Oh, could I?"

Lady Jenny's smile was sudden and mischievous, though her tone was demure. "I think I can arrange it with the Dean."

On the first Sunday after school had resumed, Orlando, Nate, Geoffrey, and Randall were invited to Chellisford Hall for Sunday dinner. Lady Jenny and Alice met them at the cathedral with the sleigh, and they all rode out through the glittering landscape to the large, half-timbered manor house. The boys were speechless as they swept up the long carriage drive, past the snow-covered garden, to the imposing front steps. Alice led them into the large entrance hall.

"Good Lord," said Orlando, gazing around the hall in amazement. There were two suits of armor standing at attention by the foot of the stairs, and an enormous tapestry with a unicorn on it covered one of the walls. "We should have named you Cat — you surely do land on your feet! Is the rest of this place as wonderful?"

Alice nodded. "Even better. Lady Jenny has all sorts of interesting things. After dinner, I'll show you the music room. She collects musical instruments and has some really beautiful ones. But listen: I received a letter from my old singing teacher in London, Master Hunnis. He said a lot of things, but I'll read you the important part." She unfolded a sheet of crackling paper, found her place, and began to read. " 'I spoke with the Queen, as I told you I would. She was furious, and was determined to bring the murderers of your father to justice. As it happened, a day or so after I spoke with her, Sir Roderick Donne came back to Court from Yorkshire. As soon as he determined the lay of the land, as it were, he approached Her Majesty and tried to persuade her to pardon him and Crofton in exchange for your safe return. I would have given a great deal to be an observer at that interview; Her Majesty has an impressive temper, though she controls it well. She told Sir Roderick she would consider his proposal once you were safely in her hands. Then word arrived from Father Boyce that you were safe. Sir Roderick was arrested and will be tried for murder and kidnapping. Lord Crofton and Father Cooper have both escaped to the Continent, but should they ever return to England, the Queen is determined to punish them.' "

The boys whistled. "I just hope they try to come back," Geoffrey said hotly. *"Then* we'll see justice done!"

"Well," Alice said, "I wish they had all been caught. It isn't fair that two of them should escape punishment. But come on. You have to meet Bertram, and then we'll eat."

"Who's Bertram?" they asked.

"He's the Earl — Lady Jenny's son. He's four. I promised I'd bring you up to the nursery and introduce you."

After the requisite introductions, Alice and her guests sat down to dinner. The food was superb: a fine mushroom soup, some broiled perch, a spiced ham, countless vegetables and side dishes, and for dessert a pound cake that all but melted in the mouth. After the meal, Alice showed them around; then they settled in the library to lounge in front of the enormous fireplace.

"Well," Randall said enviously, "you sure have it soft, Pup."

"Soft?" she demanded, laughing. "With old Bennett heaping the Latin on and Barnstable and Kenton each wanting me to practice fifteen hours a day?"

"But you get along with her, don't you?" Orlando asked. "Lady Jenny, I mean."

Alice nodded. "Lady Jenny is *wonderful*. You know, she was a friend of my father's, a long time back, and she's not stuffy at *all!* I really like it here. She's going to get me my own horse, once spring comes, and everything! And Bertram's not bad for a little kid. Besides, the food is first rate."

"That's the really important part," Geoffrey agreed. "See? I told you it would work out," he added, smiling beatifically.

"I'm really glad for you, Pup," Nate added. "And it's great you can still study with us. But how did that happen? I didn't think they were going to let you."

"Well, they weren't," she admitted. "But Lady Jenny went to work on the Dean and talked him round." They all shook their heads in amazement.

"That takes talent," Randall commented. "And speaking of talent, Pup, we really miss you in the choir."

Alice nodded more soberly. "That's the only part that's too bad. But —"

"Listen, everyone," Geoffrey broke in. "I've just had

a brilliant idea. Why don't you ask Lady Jenny to go to work on Father Boyce about the choir? I'd bet she could talk him into letting you sing with us."

Alice grinned at him. "We're way ahead of you, Geoffrey — for once! I was just going to say that Lady Jenny persuaded Father Boyce that it's vital to my education that I sing *rehearsals* with you."

The boys cheered. Geoffrey nodded, satisfied. "Then it's only a matter of time."